MW00717209

Mama's Diary

To Casandra,

A wonderful woman,
Faith, Hope, and Love Always
God Bless You.

Bridget

Mama's Diary

Bridgette D. Williams

Mama's Diary

Bridgette D. Williams

Published By:
KPG Book Publishers
(a division of Kingdom Publishing Group, Inc.)
P.O. Box 3273, Richmond, VA 23228
www.kingdompublishing.org

Library of Congress

©2011 by Bridgette D. Williams

ISBN: 978-0-9839090-7-1

Cover design: John Price

All Rights Reserved.
No part of this book may be reproduced.
This book or parts thereof may not be
reproduced in any form, without written
permission of the author except as provided by
the United States of America copyright law.

Printed in the United States of America.

Dedication

In memory of three lovely roses:

The Rose of Faith, my sister, Karen Williams Browne

The Rose of Hope, my dearest friend, Lyndsay Caraballo Ortiz

The Rose of Love, my grandmother Sarah Patrick Love

Acknowledgements

I give thanks to God the Father, Son, and Holy Spirit for salvation, deliverance, and every spiritual and natural gift.

Thanks to my family and parents, Welford L. Williams and Willie Mae Williams for your love and support.

Special thanks to the first people who read this book, my father and sister Winifred.

Thank you Bishop Grover, Pastor Scott, Pastor Pat, Pastor Kelley and the Lighthouse Christian Center Family for teaching me to use the gifts Father has given me and supporting every project I've managed.

Thank you Nina Wells, Leon Wells and the staff of Kingdom Publishing Group for helping me share the message of Mama's Diary to all who will *listen*.

Special thanks to my daughter, Imani Joy, for always believing in me, praying for me and encouraging me especially when no one else is around.

Very special thanks to my best friend and sister, Deaconess Rita Lanzillo, for telling me that I would write the message of Mama's Diary to minister God's love to many seeking hearts.

Table of Contents

Prologue

"My Little Garden"

Gazing at my little garden, I wait patiently, praying for the fruits of our works to grow. For thirty-six years we have done all that was required to produce: planting the seed, watering it, and warming it with the purest love. My time has come to stop working the garden and see what becomes of these three lovely rosebuds. Now I just pray, as Henry and I have done for the last twenty years. You see, parents never stop loving their children and when they pass on, they can only hope that the buds will blossom.

On Friday, June 12, 1987, my loving husband breathed for the last time on earth. I was not there when it happened and for the rest of my mortal life, I wished that I were. On that day, Farlinda, my oldest daughter had just come home from her last day of school for the year. My sweet sixteen was at the top of her class and her teenage world. The equation of life is simplified in the mind of an adolescent. Just add popularity to freedom and you have it. A friendly and kindhearted disposition landed my star child a multitude of friends. Henry gave her the freedom. But on that day, my sweet Farlinda discovered the body of her freedom giver, lifeless in the family room.

The day had been warm and humid. The clouds drizzled cool rain from mid-morning until after three o' clock and the temperature rose from the low seventies to mid

1

eighties. For us Virginians, this was quite a comfortable day for late spring. For Shantise, my hyperactive three-year old, it was heaven. She would find every water puddle in the Paper Store parking lot, between the exit and my Caravan, to "stomp out." For every occasion, even the most meaningless, Shantise would create a song. There were songs for waking up, eating breakfast, and even taking a bath. One time I heard her singing from the tub, "Wash my, wash my little ath, Wash my, wash my little ath, Wash my, wash my little ath, gip do my lou my dawling!" I screamed out to the guilty party responsible for the lyrics, "Henry! Don't teach my baby that word!" He thought it was cute, but with a sheepish grin, he promised never to teach her to swear again. Yes, my Shantise loved to sing. She was the loudest singer of the birthday song at her own birthday party. She sang for the moon and she even sang herself to sleep every night. On this wet day in June, she sang to the water puddles as she stamped them out, "We gonna domp! _ _ All night_ _ in da naybahoo, in da naybahoo_ _ _Domp!"

On the last "Domp!" I whisked Shantise from a puddle of something that looked like cream soda with foam around the edges. Placing her into the car seat, I lamented "Oh, God no! Why my baby Lord? Oh Jesus, look at my baby! My baby!" I had tried to save her from it. God knows I did. Unfortunately, the puddle appeared before my eyes about a half of a second before she began to "Domp in da naybahoo." Her foot landed in the largest puddle on the lot and it was made of urine. My baby's shorts, legs and socks were now drenched with water and someone's disgusting waste!

My desperate search between and under seats proved to be futile in finding a towel or paper napkin. I never took a diaper bag on short trips and Paper Store was only ten minutes from the house. There was no way she would go home in this condition. After securing her in the seat, I decided to stop in the general store for some baby wipes, a towel, lotion, rubber gloves and a carpet cleaning set. One of the shopping bags would be the seat cover and the other our makeshift hazardous material container for the shorts and socks. As I fastened my seat belt, I heard a soft voice within me that said, "Go home." Two minutes later, my van was parked in front of Dollar General.

It only took a few minutes to purchase everything on the emergency list. As I cleaned Shantise, a sensation of anxiety overwhelmed me. "Go home!" the voice repeated louder. No, no I shrugged it off with reason. Gretchen is home from school and Henry's in the home office balancing the budget. Farlinda's school bus should be dropping her off in a minute and everything is normal. "Go home now!" it screamed to me. "OK, OK in a minute!" Fighting anxiety and urine, I cleaned the car seat, and then placed a shopping bag on it. The soiled socks and shorts were placed into the other bag as planned. A few spots on the carpet were scrubbed and fifteen minutes later, Shantise was again secured in the car seat.

As I turned the corner to my street, I saw a two police cars and an ambulance in front of my house. Farlinda was sitting on the front lawn crying bitterly as she clutched Gretchen's sleepy thin frame in her arms. "Oh Lord no" disbelief and shock overwhelmed me, as I witnessed a body completely covered by a white sheet on a stretcher being rolled out of my house. "Henry!" my voice filled the minivan. Recklessly, I parked in the street and ran to the stretcher with my half dressed baby girl on my hip.

A woman police officer gently placed her hand on my shoulder and asked if I was Mrs. Silva. I nodded my head, "Yes." She then explained to me that my husband had died of a heart attack and the rescue workers had done all that they could. "I'm so sorry ma'am there just wasn't enough time to save him." My whole body shook in pain and a silent wail came from the deepest part of my soul. The only sound I made had come from the tiny puffs of hot air forced through my sore throat. Officer Kemp peeled my clenched fist from the sheet, which covered Henry's body.

We buried Henry that Wednesday. The next morning during breakfast, the girls and I had a conversation about what had happened. It was not until last month that I remembered having that time of sharing. The girls wanted to know all about the pathology of a heart attack and, very delicately, I explained it. Filled with guilt, I told them about the voice I heard three times about coming home. Before I could indulge myself further into my pity party, Gretchen began to sob, "I shouldn't have taken a nap. If I was awake, I could have helped Daddy." Immediately, Farlinda consoled, "But Grete, didn't you say Daddy gave you medicine for your allergy when you came home sneezing? Benadryl always makes you sleep. Do not blame yourself for that. And Mama, just because you were not there when Daddy had the heart attack, does not mean it was your fault that he died. I heard the police officer say there was not enough time to save him. So what could you have done if you had been there when I was or even a few minutes sooner?" I was about to answer, but was cut off before I could make the first sound of my rebuttal. "We all hurt enough by losing him. Let's not make things worse by adding guilt too." Wisdom had spoken. She pardoned Gretchen and me, and then challenged us to do the same for ourselves. Between comments and questions, the girls prepared, set, and cleaned up Shantise's breakfast. Pampered by her assistants, Shantise performed her "Eating my toast song." Little did I know, on that day my daughters had developed feelings and beliefs that shaped the rest of their lives. Farlinda became a queen, Gretchen a martyr, and Shantise, a star.

The queen ruled in her school, among her siblings and in her father's heart. Farlinda's peers described her as popular, friendly and most likely to become famous. I read all of that in the articles and messages written in her yearbook. She was captain of the School Spirit Team, an editor for the paper, a softball player and the Spring Dance Queen. On the surface, she conducted herself democratically, but in reality reigned as a dictator. Farlinda's kindness and ability to appear as a fair negotiator won over the hearts of her subjects. All of my daughters were Daddy's girls, but Farlinda was by far his favorite. He loved her energetic and happy spirit. She was smart, responsible, obedient and a very persuasive representative for herself and her sisters. A cancelled or postponed family activity was magically reinstated after he had a short conversation with her. Gretchen, having suffered from middle child syndrome, quickly learned the secret to getting her own wishes granted. She just gave her "No's" to Farlinda and asked her to have Daddy fix them. Even as young as three years old, Shantise knew about Farlinda's power and called her "Mommy." Of course, I have always been "Mama."

The martyr fought silently for my attention and Henry's affection. Neither of us purposely neglected to give Gretchen the tenderness she starved for. We just seemed to have misplaced it. Henry was so careful to lead Farlinda during those critical teen years, fearing that her peers would easily draw her away. He took for granted that by Gretchen being a child, she was happy and had no problems. Whenever she did something noteworthy, Henry would give her a warm smile, say "Good girl Gretchen," give her a pat on the back and think that she was fine. What Gretchen really needed was to hear him brag about her accomplishments and give her a big bear hug. Looking back, I focused a lot of my energy on keeping up with my three-year-old, Shantise. At the time, she was extremely busy, too busy for day care. When she was two, I had to quit my job to keep her at home. My friends who taught in school, used to shake their heads thinking she would get the diagnoses in a few years. Gretchen often tried to be Mama's assistant with the baby. When helping, she talked with me about everything that was on her heart. I am sure she thought I never listened, because I was always doing something during those times. My responses often sounded like "Yes Baby. No. That is a shame. Just try harder." At the time, I really thought I was a good listener. Oh my sweet child, if I could only do it again the right way. Instead of demanding her needs by acting out, Gretchen tried to be perfect. She behaved well in school and always had a star beside her name in the Children's Church reader's board. Masking her feelings and fulfilling the needs of others, the martyr was born at twelve years old.

For the next six years, our whole lives changed! Minus a father, I had to work two jobs: a regular Monday through Friday from eight to four and a part-time Wednesday through Saturday evenings. Unfortunately, my girls had to step up to become my little women. On those nights, Farlinda and Gretchen took turns with babysitting Shantise and cooking dinner. My sweet Farlinda missed most of her junior and senior activities because she was at home taking care of family business. My dear Gretchen lost a good portion of her high school social life for the same reason. By the grace of God, my daughters were honor students and had both earned full scholarships to college.

To say the least, they entered a realm beyond joy when they left home.

Now let me update you on who my rose buds are today. Farlinda is what Whitney Houston sang about in the nineties, "Every Woman." She runs a very successful small business, "Farlinda's Fragrances." It is a pretty little place in that new upscale mall in the west end. She lives in a cozy suburban neighborhood that looks a lot like Wisteria Lane. In her very full house are her two children, one on the way and Shantise has an apartment in her basement. One more person lives there, the grown child, Marshall Taylor. He is Farlinda's "common law husband" and father of the children. She became pregnant with their first child, Raine, during her senior and his junior year of college. Marshall immediately dropped all of his classes and got a job at Big Fat Burger to support his new family. After his second year out of school, he re-enrolled part time, but he also changed his major from education to sociology. For the next ten years, he took a class here and there and changed his major again to criminal justice. He should do well with that, because it is a crime and shame that his "wife" supports him. She earned her degree, gave birth to Florin, started her own business and became the breadwinner of the house. I truly believe that Marshall has been afraid of failing in a career, so becoming a professional student became his haven. That boy should have finished college for the fourth time by now! Well the good news is he just worked his way up the burger ladder to senior cashier.

You know my Gretchen never felt that her life was special beyond her ninth year when Shantise was born. To make up for all of the "life" she missed, Gretchen has become a high achiever. I do not have a problem with her success, but the motive behind it disturbs me. She is a program designer in a computer company who makes the brain for home appliances and office machines. Her very handsome salary affords her a luxurious downtown apartment in an exclusive tower, two expensive cars and a wardrobe to die for. Gretchen is in a few non-committed relationships with men that I probably would not trust with a dog. When she is not working or dating, she is pampering herself with jewelry, vacations, and days at the spa. Gretchen loves her family dearly, but she can never seem to find the time to spend with them. I guess she has spent enough time taking care of family business and now, every minute belonged to Gretchen.

Last year, the supernova thought it was time she moved out of Mama's house to live on her own. Farlinda, being a natural mother, immediately stepped in to help emancipate Shantise. She had spoiled her youngest sister as much as Henry and I did. Understanding that the star had no money but big dreams, she transformed the basement of her home into an apartment. Farlinda had it fully furnished as the perfect pad for the artist Shantise was becoming. She believed that her baby sis would be inspired to follow her dreams in the right atmosphere.

Shantise has something my other two daughters lack and that is faith for a better tomorrow. Farlinda has given up on moving forward with Marshall and Gretchen's low self-esteem has finally begun to surface. Like a child expecting a visit from Santa Claus, Shantise has no doubt that anything is possible. After working ten hours in Stars Video Store, she comes home to perfect her skills in singing, rapping and dancing. My only concern for her is that she has faith in a God whom she does not know.

Today is Sunday, May 13, 2007, Mother's Day. My daughters are coming to my house... not for a visit, but to read my will. It has been a week since my burial and the queen is quite eager to put another painful experience behind her.

I am certain that my rose buds will blossom, but they need just one more drop of water. So, I have completed my last will in a book, my diary.

Chapter I
Farlinda

7:30 AM

A pink satin Maternally Yours nightgown tossed side to side beneath the sheet covering her bed. Every inch of it was filled with the restless mahogany body of an African American queen. The face of Shari Belafonte's long lost twin grimaced from the discomforts of sleeping with an active fetus turning in her abdomen. In times of wellness or illness, abundance or poverty, serenity or discord, Farlinda's aura remained regal. Though her skin was much darker than Shari's, it glowed the same way. Her long black hair was tightly braided. Adorned with shells, the braids hurt! Everything hurt! Her sides hurt. Her back hurt. Her swollen feet hurt as she ran faster away from the mud covered creature in her dream. The intuitive queen knew this experience was a nightmare, but waking up challenged her. She fought hard to free her mind and won!

With a jolt she raised from her bed, curious but not panicked. Her eyes alert, intense, showing no signs that she had just awakened. Then shifting them from side to side, she looked for the source of acrid fragrance seeping into her room. "Marshall" she whispered, "Marshall, what's that smell?" He turned his body towards her revealing the Cheshire cat grin on his face, "That's your breakfast my queen." Suddenly, two round faces popped up from Marshall's side of the bed. It was Raine, their fifteen-year-old son, and Florin, their eight-year-old daughter, singing out of tune with the other, "Happy Mother's Day!"

Raine did not look like either of his parents. The only resemblance he had was the flawless deep dark skin he shared with his mother. All other features were erased by the overtones of Down's Syndrome. His chubby body was a lot smaller than those of his peers. The tight curly black locks and his usual playful expression made him the perfect image of a baby angel. His sister was the female version of Marshall. Both had caramel skin, warm brown hair and hazel eyes. Marshall's hair was cut close, but his daughter wore braided ponytails. Florin, named after a golden coin, was slender and very athletic. From the age of three, she played a sport in every season. Today, she and her brother explored the new "sport" of cooking.

Twenty minutes earlier, Marshall had coached the children through preparing their first home cooked meal for Farlinda's breakfast. Their kitchen counter had been covered with an assortment of bowls, spoons and spices normally baked in cakes and pies. Some of the bowls were partially filled with brown sugar, nutmeg, ginger, baking powder and cinnamon. One of the bowls had two beaten eggs, a pinch of flour, sugar and all spice. This would be the dip for French toast. In the center of the mess was a lukewarm bowl of over salted, lumpy grits, smothered with butter. The children carefully peeled slices of bacon out of the packages and handed them to the cook. Gently Marshall placed them on the hot skillet atop their range. He helped the slow cooking bacon progress by adding a little left over grease from last night's fish fry.

13

He used a little more of the grease on the baking pan for the biscuits. The children coated two of the biscuits with a creamy spread of butter mixed with all of the other spices on the counter. Cleverly, they had discovered how to make "sweet rolls" from the same can of biscuit dough.

Smiling appreciatively, Farlinda thanked them for the lovely Mother's Day meal, "Oh my babies, you shouldn't have..." And she meant just that, they should not have. "Marshall, you guys didn't have to go through all of the trouble of cooking for me. A breakfast combo from Big Fat Burger would have been just fine." The children's eye shot at his face and the pleading began, "Daddy can we have a combo?" they begged. Farlinda took advantage of the distraction from her face to send Marshall a secret message. She winked her eye, requesting an escape from the cellblock F combo. He did not get it. "Baby you eat and enjoy your home cooked meal and the kids and I'll eat that fast food junk!" Marshall and the children's happy faces beamed with pride as Farlinda reluctantly placed a spoon of cold grits in her mouth. Slowly she chewed the pungent lumps of mush while masking her grimaces and salt tremors as signs of pleasure. "The bacon must be better than this," she thought. It looked well done, so she took another chance and bit a piece. "Oh My God!" she said to herself, "This bacon tastes like it's been in the ocean!" Quickly she grabbed a sweet roll to get rid of the taste, but to her surprise, it was fishy too! Most unfortunately, it would take a while to swallow the great chunk she had bitten.

Florin was immediately impressed by her mother's appetite, "Good job Mommy! You took a big girl bite! See Raine, she likes the sweet roll too! And I made the frosting all by myself and Mommy loves it!" Florin continued to brag as tears formed in the corners of her mother's eyes. Painful tears! "Oh baby, you don't have to cry. It was no problem for us to do this." Marshall added, "Happy Mother's Day. We love you."

"Wait!" A voice wailed from downstairs. "Don't eat that stuff Farlinda! It smells like old burnt fish!" Shantise burst into the room. She was the younger, taller image of Farlinda. Other than sharing the same facial features, Shantise was her opposite. Farlinda, queen of the house, was content with her influence over her family and business, but Shantise wanted the world. The soon to be mega star had "the faith to be or do anything" and that would be her message to young people. When the foul aromas from the kitchen reached her bedroom, she proved her faith and became a superwoman! "Marshall don't feed my sister that mess. You want the baby to come out with fins and scales?" Farlinda laughed, "It's okay Tise. The biscuits are good. Try one." Shantise snatched the biscuit from her outstretched hand and sniffed it. Appalled by the scent, she smirked a tight grin at Marshall and whispered in his ear, "If you don't buy my sister and her unborn child a meal suitable for human consumption, I will have you put behind bars for their death! Now fix that Mr. Wannabe Attorney!" "Dang Tise, I didn't know it was that bad!" he whispered back. Embarrassed by his poor cooking skills, he remembered why years ago he was taken off the grill at work. "Kids meet me down stairs. We're going out to get breakfast." The children cheered and rushed out of the room without caring if their mother ate another bite. Farlinda raised her five foot three pear to the top of her toes to kiss Marshall. To meet her gesture, his six foot four beanpole of a body bent over to allow their lips to peck. Immediately following his disappearance, Farlinda rushed to the bathroom to purge the greasy mess from her belly. Shantise followed her closely to help.

Marshall grabbed his cell phone from his pocket and pressed the code for Big Fat Burger. Rushing down the stairs, he spoke to his faithful co-worker, "Ace, I'll be there in ten minutes. Can you have five breakfast combos ready for me? It's a Mother's Day emergency!" "You got it babe. Want Inez to pick up some flowers or candy for her too?" Ace offered. "No that's okay man. I have a real surprise for her tonight. It's something big!" Marshall gloated with pride, "See You soon." He turned off the phone and ushered the children out of the front door.

After giving her sister a warm towel for her face, Shantise began cleaning the bathroom. She decided to do a thorough job, considering that there were some unclean places that Farlinda's seven and a half month belly would not allow her to reach. She insisted to be left alone in doing this task and that the queen sit and talk with her. "Farlinda, why don't you just tell Marshall that he can't cook?"

Shantise reasoned. "I tried to give him a hint, without the kids knowing, but sometimes he can be so thick! He was so excited and caught up in the home cooked meal; he couldn't see my most obvious facade." Farlinda shook her head not believing she had once again hidden her true feelings from him. Now sitting on her bedside, she sat quietly pressing the wrinkles in her comforter repeatedly with her hands. Her thoughts carried her far and away, as Shantise continued to scold her from the bathroom about Marshall and the kids.

Farlinda's mind carried her back to when she used to assert her every thought sometimes to the extreme of controlling. Every detail of her life and Marshall's had to follow a sensible pattern she had created. Because Farlinda had only one semester left of college following the birth of Raine, she would naturally get her degree first. Around the same time, Marshall began doubting his career choice. Taking a year off to find himself and support his family was naturally the right thing to do according to the queen. After giving birth to Raine, she quickly learned how to "share" the power with Marshall. She had to after all. It would have been impossible for her to finish school, start a business and care for a new baby without his help along her side. Farlinda spent a lot less time pushing her "husband" to finish school and more into shaping her family and career. This suited her soul mate like a tailored Armani. Building a business and stabilizing the home front naturally took priority for Marshall too.

Their life was simple and mostly painless. Farlinda made all decisions concerning the family; where they would live, how to raise the children, where and who they would worship and how to manage their finances. Marshall always gave his seal of approval upon each change and when he was not sure, the queen very skillfully persuaded him to do what was right. Sometimes the benefits of surrender left him breathless.

When Farlinda was pregnant with Raine, Mama strongly encouraged her to get married. She often shared her old-fashioned views on family and religion. These talks bored her and Marshall to no end, but respectfully they listened to the same old stuff. Each time she closed with the dreaded question, "Marshall what are you going to do with your life?" Wanting the best for her daughter and grandchild, she had to know the plans of the future breadwinner. Would he stay and provide? What would he do after getting his degree? Would he leave Farlinda without a mate and the baby fatherless? Mama just had to know these things. She had her would be son in law all figured out. He was a boy in every kind of a way: insecure, indecisive, and easily influenced. This boy needed a home for stability and comfort. His responsibilities would be to baby sit during the day and contribute a portion of his salary to the household account. He would save a smaller portion to pay for a college class here and there, that is, when he felt like taking one. Marshall would stay on this course for the rest of his life, unless the queen demanded that her grown child grow up. Farlinda and her soul mate were aware of these beliefs, but again they respected her with silence.

Over the years, Farlinda and Marshall listened to Mama's sermons about God, Jesus, Moses and a whole lot of other "dead" people. Though they never went to Mama's church, they knew that they had to find something to believe in. On Florin's second birthday, they would find some answers.

The Taylor-Silva house was humming with Florin's toddler friends, her cousins and other relatives. Mama, known to the children as "Mama Silva," worked her usual post during great gatherings. In the sunroom, she became one with a rocking chair. She draped it with a soft worn quilt she had made and given to Farlinda as a child. Looking the part of an authentic storyteller, Mama captivated an audience of children and adults. Her short thin body was covered in a burnt orange caftan. Chunky brass jewelry and thong sandals complimented the African print in her outfit. Mama, known to the adults as "Justine," had long thick kinky gray hair. Her do was a cluster of box-braids, twisted into a simple bun drawn to the back of her head. Justine's golden brown face was sporadically marked with a few fine lines. Her almond shaped green eyes were gentle, warm and forever piercing through a pair of half-knit gold framed glasses. Her blushed high cheeks, full lips and L-shaped nose gave her the look of being biracial; African American and Eastern Native American. This tiny doll-like woman told the most fascinating old tales about her ancestors. Some of them were passed down through her family from six generations back. Her other stories were from the Bible. Without altering the integrity of the content, each of her stories had a little something extra added for excitement. Shantise labeled the extra as "Mama's Flava."

In the playroom and den, Farlinda, Gretchen, and Shantise were busy entertaining their guests with food and games while Marshall played catch up with several friends. His second cousin, Nadine, came with her husband, Caleb, and three-year-old daughter, Brittany. Marshall had always admired Nadine for her intelligence and her ability to know make life "work" for her instead of being "victimized" by the opposite. Even being married with a child Nadine did not lose this quality, but seemed to have matured in it. After listening to about a half an hour of Marshall's murmuring, Caleb gave him a book that would change his life. It was a book explaining the basics of Scientology. Upon receiving it, Marshall thought, "Humph, a book on religion. Farlinda is so much better at discerning this kind material. She was raised in a religious house." He shared it with her that night and something happened.

The book was perfect. It gave Marshall and Farlinda a hope for an even better life. In just a few chapters, they learned how wonderfully they were made and that they had the ability to deal with anything that came their way. The best part was finding that the answers were to be found by just a short excavation into the psyche. To Mama their new life was a door opening to the truth, but there was more to be found. To Farlinda and Marshall, it was a complete blessing!

In the spring of 2004, everything changed. Unknown to Mama, Marshall made up his mind on what to do with his life. Without attending his commencement ceremony or any activity recognizing the achievement, he had earned a bachelor's degree in sociology and political science. Promoted to manager at Big Fat Burger, he began to work the day shift and at night, he went to law school. Farlinda's Fragrances opened in late May and Mama was diagnosed with uterine cancer.

"Farlinda, I don't know how you do it!" Shantise continued to scold her sister. There was no response, only wrinkle pressing. "Hello, earth to Farlinda! Come in, Farlinda!" She sighed, "I'm still here Shantise, just barely though." "What do you mean, just barely here? What is wrong? Are you still sick?" She sighed again, "No I've been thinking about everything that's happened the last few years. Just last year, you moved in and now you are sending CDs to record companies. Things are really looking up for my baby sis." Farlinda stopped pressing and fixed her gaze on the striped comforter pattern. Closing her wet eyes and shaking her head "no," she managed to exhale her fears. "I don't know what I'm gonna do when you sign on with someone. I feel as if I will be lost without having you here, fussing and keeping us all in line. You will be in New York or L.A. and I will be here stuck with our snooty sibling.

Every year, since she started working for Home Tech, Gretchen has had less and less time for us. Then there is Mama. Three years ago, she started chemotherapy and had the hysterectomy for uterine cancer. Everything was fine until this March when she came out of remission and now she is gone! Our mama, our strength, our light, our rock is gone. Only two weeks ago, she was telling Raine and Florin one of her crazy ole stories and now she's history." She wept openly, "Shantise, I don't know if I'm strong enough for this. I have always had so much control of my life and even my emotions. But I could not control death. I cannot get the real Gretchen back. My kids are as active as you were when you were little and my marathon engagement seems to have no end. Marshall acts like he has some kind of marriage phobia and I feel sick again!" Following her into the bathroom for the second time, Shantise tried to console her. "Farlinda, stop. You are carrying too much now. No, you cannot change the past or the future, but you can change right now. Let's just deal with one thing at a time. You feel sick and we are gonna take care of that. I'll get the ginger ale and you promise me to never eat another dish cooked by Marshall and or those wild kids!" She went to Farlinda's bedroom mini refrigerator, pulled out a can of ale and waited on her to finish the purging.

After flushing, washing her hands and face, Farlinda made a plan. "We're going to read Mama's will today," she declared firmly. The queen was back. "Oh no, please it's Mother's Day. Just stay home and relax" Shantise whined.

Then she remembered something else, "Wait a minute Farlinda! Didn't you take care of her final business with arranging the funeral and burial?" Farlinda sighed and answered, "Mama had a prepaid funeral and burial plot. I only had to put the program together. We have an appointment with the lawyer to read the will tomorrow. Actually, she had two wills. She said the lawyer has the legal document and there is also an informal will just for us. Today is the perfect day to read the informal will. We need to remember our mother and the best way is to read her words that she wrote for us. Tise, we gotta do this." She persisted while taking the can of ginger ale, "We can go after you finish working this evening. You should be there around five?" "Well, ok for me, but what about Gretchen? She is nearly impossible to catch on a Sunday or any day! Let's just wait until tomorrow as planned and she'll be there for sure." The queen rebutted, "No Tise. Today! We must read it today and Gretchen will come. I can feel it in my spirit. Today is the right day." Lacking enough wit and energy to fight an expert debater, Shantise surrendered the argument. "Alright then you call her. I can never persuade Grete to do anything. I am leaving in a few minutes to see Velvet. She wants to introduce me to some guys in the music business. They are interested in recording and managing us. Call me if you need anything." She kissed her sister on the forehead and went to the basement for her keys and purse.

Chapter II

Shantise

8:15 AM

Farlinda and Marshall had made the front half of the basement apartment into a lounge and mini recording studio. The studio was located to the right upon entering. A semi-circle soundproof wall with a very large glass window in its center encased it. They chose a contemporary décor for the lounge. The walls were plastered with photographs and abstract paintings of musicians. Black and white marble tile covered the entire front half of the apartment. Her black suede sofa and love seat matched the stools at the bar. Her bar was used as her dining area and behind it was the kitchen. The back half of the apartment is her bedroom and bathroom. Shantise decorated this half of the diva pad in a funky 1970's style. The authentic furniture, curtains and lamps were carefully refurbished by one of Farlinda's friends who sold antiques. This apartment and her car was all that she had. Added to that, she had dreams, big dreams.

Shantise used her earnings to pay for dance classes, voice training, and to maintain her car and urban wear wardrobe. "Not bad for a person of my age," she often told herself. Never comparing her lifestyle with her college graduate sisters, the diva had never doubted that her breakthrough was just around the corner. By no means did she consider herself religious or spiritual. Shantise went to church about eight to ten times per year. Being all holy and sanctified as her mother was the life for old people and nerdy young followers. She did not have the time or the personality to be a bench warmer. Life had to go on. Jesus loved her and she knew this truth without a doubt. She trusted that God had her back in every move she made and that He would be the source of her success.

The keys to her 2007 Sunlight Silver Mazda RX-8 Coupe Sport were found in the same place where she always stored them. Each time she parked, they were tucked in the side compartment of her Roca Wear purse. She grabbed her bag, dashed up the stairs and out of the side door, which led to the driveway. Marshall had just parked beside her car and held a Big Fat Burger bag out of the window. Grasping the bag by her middle finger and thumb, she responded in Morticia Addams' voice "Thank you Thing." He laughed and waved her off, "Go to work Tise!"

Shantise knew she was blessed when she sat on her black leather seats. While backing out, she began to think about all that God had given her. She was grateful for her talent, possessions and mostly her family. Her mother had raised her Gretchen and Farlinda, the best that she could without their father. Justine worked hard to insure that her daughters never lacked in anything. Though she did not have the time or money to support their every interest, she managed to indulge each of them on their one favorite thing. After their father's passing, Farlinda batted out her frustrations and disappointments on the softball diamond. Gretchen went to Girl Scout meetings on Saturday mornings. Shantise was treated to the latest R& B and Hip Hop CDs.

At the end of the driveway, she backed out to the left and after a brief pause, shifted into first gear. The second blessing came to her mind; it was her oldest sister. She had provided her the perfect dwelling for her to nurture her talents. It was nothing like her old room in Mama's house with paper-thin walls. She did not have to worry about hearing a bang on her door followed by a command to turn the music down. Shantise shifted into second gear and a smile appeared on her face as she celebrated having the gift of freedom. It quickly disappeared when she remembered that there was no one to run any from anymore. There was no one to tell her that she needed to have a relationship with the Lord. There was no one to tell her to think carefully about her future and be more selective with whom she calls a friend. The nagging was over. How could she go on without "The Voice" (her mother's thoughts and wisdom) to fight?

Shantise, unlike her sisters, challenged the voice that her mother called "guidance" and she called it "a pain." By the age of seventeen, she had had enough. The real diva had begun to surface. Sundays had become a day that she chose her own activity. In the morning, she would either sleep in or report to work. She had spent enough of her life going to church every Sunday morning. Occasionally would be enough. The young adult choir and youth sang on the fourth and fifth Sunday. On some of those days, Shantise showed up to enjoy "good music" or tease one of her church friends while they sang. In the afternoon, she may or may not eat dinner at home. Meals could be consumed on her way to work, on a break, late night in front of the television, or even in the home of one of her crazy friends. She did not have to sit down at a table to be bored by the same old wild tales and "wisdom" from The Voice. Her haven was in the basement of her emancipator. In this place, The Voice was silent. She shifted into third gear.

Turning the curve to enter I-295, Shantise cleared her conscience of her mother and thought about Gretchen. "Yeah Grete's got game! That's what I call success." She rubbed the healing salve of Gretchen on the wounded area of her memory. The smile returned as she shifted into fourth. Her head filled quickly with happy thoughts, sprinkled with pride and money. Good ole stuck up Grete came through for her birthday. She made a huge down payment and co-signed for the Mazda Shantise had just shifted into fifth gear. Zoom! She sped down the interstate. Her church friends, Vita and Jewel, envied this awesome machine. Vita asked the Lord why she had not been blessed with something like that. She had always been a good Christian. She even gave her tithes and offerings every week. Jewel, did not reason with God, she just came out flat ugly, "Girl, what do you need with a sports car? We are trying to get you saved and you are moving further away from the Lord. We see you at church less every year since we were seniors in high school. You hang out with the "reprobates" TJ and Velvet and now this! You are going too fast girl. I'll be praying for you." "Keep on praying sister" Shantise spoke to the memory. Her face beamed with pride as she downshifted while entering the I-95 ramp headed south toward the downtown.

Leaving the ramp, she shifted back into fifth and thought of her true friends, TJ and Velvet. She met them in the ninth grade chorus. Terrell Junior, TJ, was known as the most desired loner in high school. Having the appearance of a professional model, manners of a gentleman and the scent of Calvin Klein, TJ was "The Man." The girls trailed his path as puppies do when lured by the aroma of treats as they are trained to be house broken. Strangely, TJ was the sole member of his click. He lived safely within himself, where the music was. A hip-hop or R&B tune constantly played in his psyche and sometimes the lyrics would escape through his lips. At home, TJ created raps to soothe his broken soul from the dark past. Outwardly, his superior complex confused the "little people" who would someday be his fans. Though he was polite to everyone, he managed to keep others at arm's length from himself. In his mind, he was a star to be seen, heard, but never touched. That changed in the tenth grade when he graciously allowed two deserving females, Margaret and Shantise, into his life. This boy who survived an abusive childhood had finally accepted them as friends after a long and careful inspection of their personalities. Based upon her genuine kindness and the ability to stay out of fights and gossip, Shantise was his first friend. Margaret seemed nice, but nearly invisible. That relationship would take some time to develop. TJ could sense that she was trustworthy, but it was hard to catch up with her. She always seemed to be in a hurry to be some place. Her words were short and few.

Margaret reminded TJ of the loner he used to be. She was extremely quiet, withdrawn and very beautiful. In every season and occasion, her perfectly shaped body was covered. Her wardrobe consisted of heavy sweat suits, baggy jeans and long sleeved shirts. An instant bond was created when TJ accidentally bumped his lunch tray into her back. Discovering a most unusual tender spot as she shrieked from the pain, he knew from experience what she was hiding beneath her sweat suit and flawlessly made up face. He demanded that she eat lunch with him and Shantise. Margaret was saved that day, but not by the school counselor who her new friends had taken her to see. She was saved by the unconditional love and support they freely gave her. TJ and Shantise promised never tell a soul any of Margaret's well-protected secrets. They helped her move into a foster home near the school and visited her often. The three of them would hang out in the dining room to study and practice songs they had learned in chorus. Mr. and Mrs. Tang loved the sound of their voices filling their evenings with laughter and music. Often Shantise and TJ accepted their dinner invitations, which made Mrs. Tang very happy. It gave her the feeling of having the big family that she could never produce naturally.

One day before dinner with Margaret's family, Shantise gave TJ a low five under the table. This was her signal to alert him that she would be leaving him alone with his long time crush. After she left, TJ sung a ballad he wrote for Margaret expressing his love for her. In the song, he called her his Lady Velvet, because her voice was soft and smooth. Her new boyfriend had given her a name that she loved enough to have everyone call her by it. From that day on, she would be known as Velvet.

On weekends, Mrs. Tang took Velvet shopping for girlish clothing and had her hair done by professionals. The Tangs were the parents she had only dreamed that her natural parents would be. They were patient, gentle and very knowledgeable about the mental scars that child abuse can leave upon an individual. Quite naturally, they were grateful to witness their foster daughter blossom into a young lady. Mr. Tang dotingly referred to her as his princess. For the rest of her high school years, Velvet's image had transformed from frumpy to fabulous and her lifestyle emerged from gloom to glam. She was a happy girl for the first time in many years. One day after dinner, she told TJ that she felt like Cinderella, leaving an abusive past and finding her prince all at the same time.

TJ the model, Shantise, the star and Velvet the princess, had formed a music group well known to their school community as Top Three. Most of the engagements were hosted by teachers, their families and friends. Sometimes they were invited to sing at festivals, parties and weddings. They wrote and performed many of their own songs. TJ wrote raps and dreamy love songs. Shantise wrote some raps and choreographed their dancing. Velvet was not a songwriter; instead, she was a soulful performer, a lot like Billie Holliday. She sang rhythm and blues as though every fiber of her being had been made from it.

High school was over and Top Three's gigs were few and far between. Though not a couple any more, TJ and Velvet were good friends. They lived, but never slept together in the same house. They also worked in the same clothing store during the day. The three of them wanted desperately to rebuild their reputation as a group and be discovered by some one big. On the morning of May 13, 2007, TJ would introduce his friends to the gentlemen who would jump-start their music careers.

Shantise parked in front of the door to TJ and Velvet's townhouse. "We've changed a lot she thought to herself. I hope we can stay together and do this." TJ had the reputation of a hustler, selling bootleg videos and other hot goods to supplement his tiny income. He worked in parking lots, behind buildings and in alleys. Once he was bold enough to work in a movie theatre lot, convincing people that his $5.00 versions of the movies were perfect and a lot cheaper. Velvet had her side hustle too. She worked weekend nights for cash, waiting tables in a secret club. Shantise and TJ tried to have her disclose its name and location, but she never budged as if her life depended upon keeping it quiet. Velvet's uniforms were a collection of racy lingerie. Each night the waitresses wore the color for the evening. Not touching the wait staff was a house rule, but rarely enforced by the "security." Excessive flirting, harassment and occasional slip of the hand came with the job. The dancers were not as fortunate. Members were allowed to touch them as they tucked tips beneath the belts and straps of their costumes. Velvet hated the members of the Medallion Society, but not for their treatment of women. It was their destructive values, beliefs and influence on local politicians. She would not be quitting any time soon to give up the good pay. Velvet and TJ had been saving their hustle money for a move to Hollywood. Shantise's savings did not compare to what they had put aside. Her plan was to sell the fine furniture of her apartment and if necessary some clothing to finance her trip.

"Come in Tise!" Velvet beamed as she waved her fingers inward. "This is Chain and Mann from Orbit Records of Hollywood!" Shantise immediately felt uncomfortable in their presence. Mann appeared to have been in his early thirties, clean cut and business-like. His slim, well-toned frame stood at six feet and two inches. He had the face of a Mayan god: bronze skin, broad features, deep brown eyes, perfect white teeth, and wavy black hair. His navy stripe Burberry suit with matching tie and lavender silk shirt gave him an approachable look. Mann walked in black Gucci loafers and his steps were strong, confident and proud like those of a tycoon. Chain's demeanor and outfit radiated intimidation. His six foot-four muscular body had several scars upon it from many victories and defeats from the battles he had fought on the streets and in prison. "Gangster" was written all over his baggy white unknown designer suit. His shiny black shirt sparkled at the wrist with silver and diamond cuff links. There was no tie, but a thick silver herringbone chain dressed his wide neck. The pointed -toe black patent leather shoes matched the gloss of the chain and cuff links, but they could not compete with the shine on his bald head. Covered in smooth ebony skin, Chain's face reflected his mixed heritage of a Nigerian mother and Vietnamese father. Though he behaved like a man in his early twenties, his countenance was that of a much older person. The spokesman of this mixed matched identity had the deep voice of John Coffey from the movie Green Mile and manners of a scheming player.

TJ and Velvet were instantly impressed by their outward appearance, but Shantise was not sold as quickly. She critically observed the over excited actions of her friends. Upon every few phrases that Chain uttered, TJ moved in some kind of uncoordinated "hip hop" manner. He bounced, sucked his teeth, cursed, and threw jabs. None of these behaviors were typical of TJ. His overly active body stayed in motion to prove himself street worthy, strong and cultured enough to work with Chain and Mann. "What a fake!" Shantise thought as she watched TJ make a street fool of himself. On the other hand was Velvet. Turning off her sweet, classy manners, she became the brainless uncouth girl who waited tables in the un-named strip joint. Popping her gum loudly and adding "Oh my God!" to the end of every Hollywood promise, Velvet was in heaven.

"What up Tise? You ready to make some real money with us?" Chain asked with a broad smile and extending his hand. "We gonna get this thing moving tonight, you down with it?" She shook his hand. Besides his shark-like grin, something about him smelled fishy, like raw sardines under a sunny sky in July. "Sure" Shantise forced from the back of her throat. She began to tremble as he smiled and took a full visual inventory of her body. "Relax baby. You gonna be a star." He rubbed her chin with Brute 33 scented fingers. "Pack a few things and we'll see you back here tonight. Let's say about eight thirty." "Pack for what?" Shantise was confused. "Our trip to Hollywood!" Velvet squealed as she grabbed her trembling hands, "And we don't have to pay for it! Chain and Mann have their own plane. Oh my god, Tise, They are going to fly us to California!" That statement sent fearful chills throughout Shantise's bones. Skillfully, she masked her true feelings with jumps and cheers matching Velvet's in seemingly perfect harmony. "Oh my god what are we gonna bring?" Shantise cried with baby tears spilling from the corners of her eyes. The eleventh grade drama class had paid off in that one moment. Behaving as an unprofessional, naïve adolescent, she pretended to momentarily forget about the "opportunity" and focus on the excitement of the trip and being a star. She became the dumb-witted girl her predators had been seeking." Excuse us a minute! I need to find her an outfit!" Shantise smiled as she pulled Velvet into her bedroom.

The door slammed behind them and Shantise shoved Velvet in the corner opposite it. The smile disappeared, replaced by a tight wide-eyed glare. "Who the hell are these guys, Velvet? You don't know them and neither does TJ!" Stunned by the change, Velvet said, "TJ knows them from the parking lot at the movie theatre! He sold them twenty movies! These are not everyday guys. They work for Orbit! Aren't you excited?" "Big time guys with a private plane, buying five dollar bootleg videos in a parking lot? Come on Velvet, don't you see phony written all over them!" "See there you go Miss Bourgeois West End Diva! You won't ever be a star with your attitude!" Velvet retorted. "Don't be stupid Velvet. Just look at Chain. How many rich guys have you seen decked out in a cheap suit? His shoes squeaked on every step. The man had a scar on his face and his neck! Someone wanted to kill him! Come on, let us be real, how many classy rich guys get into fights like that? Thug is written all over him!" The stereotyping angered Velvet. "Shantise you make me sick! You see a big black guy with a few scars and you assume the worst. Girl, you look and act just like your mama. If I did not know you any better, I would call you Ms. Silva. You trust nobody!" Shantise's head dropped as she examined all of the truths in that speech. Just then, Velvet remembered Ms. Silva's recent death the second after she blasted her best friend.

"Aw, Tise, I'm sorry!" she began to cry, "I didn't mean to say..." Shantise solemnly interrupted, "No it's ok, I am like my mama. Look, I am not saying 'no' to Hollywood yet. I just need a couple of hours to figure out these guys. If they check out ok, I will be back this evening. If not, I'm calling it off." "How are you gonna do all of that and work too?" Velvet said puzzled. "I have my ways" Shantise was always vague when she went into her protective mode. They embraced each other tightly, as though it was the last time. Fear covered Velvet like a robe as she felt Shantise's vibes of suspicion.

Velvet slowly opened her bedroom door and pasted a fake smile on her lips. The three men were talking about songs and background music. Mann noticed that she had been crying but said nothing. Instead, he looked at her with deep felt compassion in his eyes. His business face turned on at the moment that Chain and TJ looked towards him. Shantise followed Velvet, still appearing to be excited and hugged her once more. "I'll be back tonight!" she sang. Again, Mann and Chain's hands were shook and TJ was kissed gently on the cheek as she exited the townhouse.

"Wait!" a voice cried out behind her. Velvet came out running to tell her one more thing. Chain and Mann were also making a quick exit to get to their next destination. "See ya tonight partna!" Chain flashed a smile at Mann as he jumped into the front passenger side of a white 1978 Monte Carlo. Its high set tires had shiny silver caps appeared to have spun to the rhythm of the loud rap music that flowed from the windows. Both girls watched Chain's grand exit with opened mouths, but only one of them was in awe. "If that's a Hollywood business man, my name is Mariah Carey!" Shantise thought. "Aw, he is so fine!" Velvet panted. Chain blew them a kiss just before his driver sped off and whipped around the corner. Neither of them noticed how Mann left, but they did enjoy the fragrance of Clive Christian 1872 that caught a breeze when he passed them. He had crossed the street and seemed to have disappeared through an alley.

Velvet was still staring at corner when Shantise snapped at her, "Wake up! Girl, what do you want? I need to go to work now!" She giggled, "I just wanted to see if the back side of Chain was as fine as the front!" "And you held me up for that!" Shantise fumed. "Yeah, I thought I'd share a little piece with you" Velvet said with a tiny punch to her shoulder. "You're a sick child and that piece is making me late for work!" she said running to her car. As she backed out of the parking space, Shantise, yelled her farewells, "Tonight, I'm bringing you some Cold Shower in a Can!" Velvet looked puzzled as she turned the car to the side. "You know... It's for de-hornification!" Shantise laughed and sped off before Velvet could retort.

"Ten minutes before nine. I think I can get to work on time," Shantise assured herself as she turned the corner. The silver Mazda zoomed through the slow Sunday morning traffic as a hungry mouse pursuits cheese in a maze. Barely missing fenders by inches, she slipped between cars to advance her distance. Several angry and startled faces glared at her as she passed them. A church van from Mt. Peace was one of the vehicles intimidated by her offensive driving. The driver looked hard at her through a closed window. Shantise could read his lips as me mouthed an appalled, "Damn!" He then pulled the van to the right to pick up his first group of churchgoers. Shantise watched this from her rear view mirror and burst out in laughter. "Sorry church boy!" Her smile faded as blue lights flashed from an unmarked police car that came from behind the van.

She pulled her car to the right side of the street and waited. The loud tooting of a horn startled her as the Mt. Peace van passed with a smiling driver and waving passengers. "I have been damned by God's servant" she reasoned. "No ma'am you damned yourself with that manic driving. May I have your license and registration, please?" As she reached in to her purse, she could smell a familiar fresh scent blowing in through her window. She turned quickly to face the origin of the scent. A fitted uniform covering a well-built body, with name Rojas on the tag was the source of her fragrance déjà vu. Her eyes caught his as she inhaled it again. "Impossible!" she whispered, frozen and staring into the same face that had disappeared through an alley between townhouse buildings. Officer Rojas smiled back and said "Possible." Shantise handed him the license and registration. She watched him stroll to his black Camaro through the side view mirror. Completely baffled, she rubbed her forehead and wondered how could

Mann change from a suit to a uniform within three minutes and be on patrol. Why was it that he did not remember her from Velvet and TJ's place?

Officer Rojas returned with her belongings and a traffic court summons. "Miss Silva, you don't have to appear in court unless you wish to contest to the justification of the arrest. You can pay the violation fine and fees by calling the phone number here." He pointed to a box with a boldly printed message in side of it. "You'll be guided through an automated system which will tell you how much to pay and where to mail it." Still bewildered about his identity, Shantise asked, "How did you do that Mann?" Mistaking the name "Mann" for the word "man," Officer Rojas suspected that she beginning to question his authority. "Excuse me ma'am? Is there a problem?" Immediately feeling his vibes, she became nervous as she answered, "No, no, no problem" she stuttered "But there is a prob... I mean, I mean... Officer, I am confused. Aren't you the same guy from Orbit Records? Like weren't you just at Velvet and TJ's" Officer Rojas's face turned red, "What was that? You said you saw me at some other place?" " Yes, yes, Velvet and TJ's! You have the same face, hair and scent. You must be Mann, unless you have a twin from California." He raised a brow and smiled a devilish grin when she said "scent." Sliding on his sunshades, he tested her, "Miss Silva, what scent am I wearing?" Shantise could identify each of the one hundred and twenty-two male fragrances that her sister sold. Without a doubt she answered, "Clive Christian 1872"

Shantise took the summons and her things from the officer who now looked as stunned as she felt. He held on to the top of her door, staring into the space above the car. *This man must think I'm crazy I'd better leave before I get into something.* "Officer, can I go now? I'm late for work." His expression changed from curiosity to amusement, "No, tell me more about the guy who looks like me" Feeling relieved to unload the enigma that danced in her mind, she told him the whole story about Chain, Mann, and the promises of stardom. Officer Rojas knuckled his head with his fist, as he appeared to have remembered something, "Oh Yes, that music man. I have been mistaken for him before, but that was years ago. Taurus Mann used to be a singer right here in Richmond before he went to Orbit. You have probably never heard of him. He was known before your time." He smiled at her and said, "Hey you're on your way to the top and Rojas is gonna give you a break." He extended his hand for the citation and she gave it back to him. "Just remember to bring me some tickets when you come back to perform in town." *Oh my god, being a celebrity has its perks! I can get used to this life style.* Shantise smiled as the reality of becoming a star had finally sunk in. Velvet was right about her. She had been cynical and foolish. What could have been two hustlers, turned out to be legitimate businessmen and what could have been a traffic ticket turned out to be nothing. "Thank you Officer Rojas." She exhaled in relief. With a wave and grin, she was on her way to Stars.

Officer Rojas returned to his car, but not as the star-struck admirer Shantise had met. This angry man tasted the bitterness of betrayal sticking to the roof of his mouth. He banged his fist on the hood of the Camaro. "When I find that player, I'll kill him!" Fragments of broken sunshades were swept to the ground.

Chapter III

Gretchen

11:00 AM

Her head bobbed to a soft reggae rhythm, as she stared hypnotized by the clear blue Caribbean. Warm sweet air surrounded her hourglass shaped bikini clad body. Gretchen extended the beach chair 30 degrees back to take in the cloudless sky. "You want another margarita my Nubian queen?" Taye Diggs asked the woman he worshipped every night. "Why not, I can't get a buzz from it and in a little while you'll be gone and I'll wake up." Taye handed her a fresh glass and smiled, "But the good news is I'll be back tomorrow night and we can pick up where we left off." They agreed upon the truth and tapped glasses, as it became their toast. Just then, a funky little ring tone interrupted their drinks.

"Taye, who is that calling you on our vacation? It better not be Angela Bassett. She is not your real girlfriend. You did get her straight on that didn't you?" "No, no it's no one. Someone probably has the wrong number. Hear the ringtone? Nothing special, it's just the funny tune I got from the service provider." *Good trick Taye, but not good enough. I do that all the time to save myself from getting caught. Only fools use special ringtones for their lovers!* Gretchen grabbed the phone and opened it, only to see the lovely face of Angela Bassett.

"It's over between you two! Now just leave him alone! He's mine now!" Gretchen grabbed her chest when the woman spoke back to her in a very familiar voice, "Grete what's wrong? Why are you yelling at me?" Taye always answered the questions in Gretchen's mind correctly because he lived there, "That is your sister on the phone. Now calm down before you speak to her again." She slowly opened her eyelids, which had been tightly closed and discovered that she was at home in her bed. The dark chocolate muscle bound figure beside her rolled over to face her. She had awakened Jamel, her favorite boyfriend. "Grete, what are you shouting about?" he asked sliding close enough to feel her body against his. Gretchen waved her hand over his lips to hush him. Shantise had been completely sold on the workaholic image of Gretchen and would have never visualized the "perfect" sister in this scene. Even though Gretchen knew that Farlinda was aware of her female player lifestyle, she kept both sisters far away from it. She maintained a man-less front in their presence: sterile, proper, and untouchable. Jamel thought that whole charade was silly but cute. He respected her wishes and sealed his lips with a grin.

"Farlinda...?" "Yes, Grete it's me, your sister, and I don't want your man!" Farlinda laughed and again asked Gretchen what was wrong. As she began to explain the recurring dream with Taye Diggs, Jamel got up to take a shower. He had heard about her dreamland lover one too many times. Jamel was disgusted by her fantasy. For the last ten months, he tried to show Gretchen how much he loved her and wanted her to be satisfied with him only. He hated having to share her with a phantom, fearing that he would never be enough for her. If he had only known that he was sharing her with a few others, the relationship would have been over. Gretchen had told him months before that she really cared for him, but she was not ready for a committed relationship. She never mentioned Malcolm, the obstetrician or Garrett, the UPS guy. Heaven forbid if he ever found out about Vaughn, the twenty two year old mail carrier who looked like Taye Diggs! Judging by their careers, Gretchen just wanted a man who could deliver.

Unlike the others, Jamel owned a construction company that built hotels, apartments and townhouses. When he inherited it from his grandfather, Jamel had firms in three states. Over the following two years, he had doubled that. He spent a lot less time in his Virginia based headquarters to physically check up on progress elsewhere. His every other weekend in town suited Gretchen perfectly. On the other weekends, Malcolm would take her on healthy retreats such as hiking, spas, or camping. Some early Saturdays or during the week after work hours, she would team up with Garrett for meals and shopping. Then there was Vaughan, the very energetic youngster who took her to the fitness center three nights per week and treated her to another work out in his apartment afterwards.

Malcolm and Vaughan, though unaware of the other's involvements, learned that their relationship with Gretchen would be short term. So, instead of becoming deeply involved, they had to accept the only woman she would allow them to have. They each enjoyed their mutual interests with her and covered their hearts with armor. Garrett, on the other hand, was an enemy to commitment. He never had moments of frustration as Malcolm and Vaughan did, wanting more but settling for less. He valued the free time with his non-committed girlfriend. He was her only boyfriend who was aware of the others in her life because only he could understand the needs of such a woman. He knew about her past, present and fantasy lovers. Garrett knew her taste in clothing, shoes, jewelry and perfumes. Though not committed to date one another exclusively, he knew all of her intimate details. On some of the non-Vaughan weeknights, she would snuggle in Garrett's arms and tell "Daddy" about her accomplishments, her dreams, and fears. In turn, Garrett would carefully listen and when she finished, he gently made love to her. She trusted the man version of herself. It was like having a twin or a very close girl friend who just happened to be a male. Sometimes she wondered about his other partner preferences because he understood women too well in her eyes.

This weekend should have belonged to Jamel but it would end hours earlier than planned. He decided to leave her with the fantasy lover and offer her the professional help she needed years ago. After he showered and dressed, he overheard Gretchen's conversation with Farlinda. "Do we have to do this today? I have plans you know" looking towards Jamel. He waved a gesture to tell her to go with her sister. "Well, ok, but let's do it quickly. Today is Mother's Day and I just cannot stand to be in her house that long. It's just too soon for this." Reluctantly, Gretchen gave in. She would miss the last few hours with the man who made her feel strong, safe and empowered. Unlike Garrett, who licked all of her wounds, Jamel taught her how to protect herself. Because of his influence, she was promoted to the Program Design Manager at work. Gretchen was falling in love, but could not admit it, not even to herself. She had loved one man in her life and in her eyes; he barely knew how to reciprocate it. Her father, Henry had invested so much of his time into Farlinda that Gretchen became a mere shadow of a daughter. Before she could grow up to take Farlinda's place, he had died. This would not happen to her ever again. From then on, there would be no man held in a special place in her heart. Though not special, each man did at least have a place in her life: Malcolm was her health guru, Vaughan was her fitness trainer, Garrett was her confidant and Jamel was her mentor.

Hanging up the phone, she ran to stop Jamel from leaving, "Baby where are you going?" "I'm going home so that you can spend some time with your family for a change. How long did you stay with Farlinda and Shantise after the funeral last week?" Jamel knew her weaknesses and he hated to see her become a victim to them. "Oh, come on Jamel please. They do not need me around. You don't know what I've been through with my family." He looked puzzled, "It couldn't have been that bad you seem to talk with Farlinda a few minutes every weekend I'm here and you bought Shantise a new car." Gretchen snapped back, "I didn't buy her a car. I gave her a down payment and co-signed. She is taking care of her own payments. Shantise is spoiled! Mama, Daddy and Farlinda spoiled her. But I will not be a part of that. I gave her something to start with, but she will have to work like the rest of us if she wants to keep it. I am just teaching her a lesson in responsibility. She does not need me. She just needed a hand. Anyone could have done that. "

"Girl you don't want to admit it, but you've got a good heart. You just give little pieces of it to the people you love as if you will mistakenly give them too much. What are you afraid of?" He embraced her and went on, "Gretchen, I don't know what happened in your past with them, but your future has got to be better. Just take a chance and open your heart to them. Let them see the real Grete, not the snotty sister you pretend to be, but this woman. This one..." He lifted her sorrowful head to look into the face of the real woman who began to weep. "You need them, they need you. Stop treating them like this and be a family." Jamel was right and Gretchen could not deny it. "I want to be myself and love them like sisters, but I don't know how." She buried her head into his chest and cried on him until his shirt was wet with tears. *Thank God. She's finally opening.*

"Gretchen, I love you. One day, God willing, we'll be married and I'll make an honest woman out of you!" They both began to laugh at the "honest" part knowing how hypocritical it sounded. It was a funny introduction into his speech, but he also meant what he said about marriage. "What I'm saying is that you have an intimacy problem." Defending herself she cut him off, "Wait a minute. I can be intimate. We just spent the night together. That was intimate! What do you want?" Gretchen knew what he wanted but feared it most of all. She knew that Jamel was the man that she should tell her secrets to. Instead, the sensitive non-committed Garrett was given that privilege. They used each other for that. Garrett knew the task of listening to a broken woman would pay off in bed most every time. Gretchen knew he was just an ear, but nothing else. She just used him to unload and never have to deal with the issues afterwards. She feared that if she ever "unloaded" on Jamel, he would take her seriously and try to help. Help was the last thing the martyr wanted. She could handle everything herself. She would use the men in her life to fill her days and nights, so that she would not have much time to think about real things. Jamel interrupted her thoughts and continued, "Each time you put down your guard another one comes up. I just want to love you without having to fight off some invisible foe. There is always something in the way. You do not let love have its way in your family. You share your affection for me with a man in your head. I just do not get it. Can you tell me what is going on with you? Do you have another man and I'm getting in the way?" Gretchen felt she would lose this good man if she answered honestly. "No there's no one." she said. Then feeling the guilt she answered again, "Well no one I'm serious with. (He thought she was referring to Taye) But Jamel you are special and I like you more than I ever wanted to. Look, I know you want more and you deserve that and in reality I want more too, but..." Her head dropped and she began to sob again.

Gretchen was tired; emotionally, mentally and physically tired. The brokenhearted martyr was tired of killing herself over the past. Indulging herself in every pleasure was beginning to play itself out. Somehow, she would have to learn how to face the ghosts of childhood bravely and put them away. She would have to deal with her fear of abandonment and loneliness, the real reason for having led a non-committed love life. Mentally, she had burned out her thought fuses, trying desperately to figure out where to begin in the rescue operation of Gretchen's soul. Her personal life had become a tangled mess of poor decisions and low self-esteem covered in pride & money. The playgirl lifestyle of juggling men combined with the stress of a demanding career left her body drained on this Sabbath morning. She had spent all of Saturday working with Jamel and few of his employees on a charity project for a poor family. They repaired a water pipe and two rooms that had been badly damaged by water. That night she went with him to a fundraiser ball for a new shelter for the homeless. Neither of them had so much fun in a great while. They drank and danced until the end, which was two o' clock in the morning. Upon entering Gretchen's bedroom, they used the remaining energy to love one another. Her eyes finally closed at five o' clock. So, now after a busy week and night, the man who loved her could see that she was indeed exhausted.

This time Jamel did not probe for more information. He carried Gretchen back to her bed, covered her with a blanket and prescribed more rest before she meet with her sister. After kissing her forehead, Jamel grabbed his jacket and headed out of the bedroom. Before leaving, he stopped in the kitchen to write her a letter. He left the letter with a business card, which read "Amelia Covington, Counselor." Amelia was the therapist he met with during his divorce, five years ago. Gretchen drifted back into sleep only a few minutes after he departed.

Three hours later, she took a shower and got ready for brunch. Gretchen combed her wavy bob with a light creamy hairdressing. She pulled it into a ponytail and put pearl clips on her ears lobes. After placing a delicate string of pearls around her neck, she smoothed bronze mineral powder on her "Justine Silva" face. She patted a bit of warm rose to her cheeks and plum berry to her lips. Then looking into a closet full of choices, finding something to wear would not be problem. Effortlessly, she transformed a beautiful girl into a model ready for the world. Her mid section growled as hunger had finally caught up with her, after a nineteen hour fast. *Where will I eat on Mother's Day without waiting an hour or two to be seated? All of the good places would probably be booked until closing. I know. I'll call Clara; she'll squeeze me in somehow.*

"GL Silva" appeared in the name box of The Pink Garden's caller ID. Clara answered on the third ring 'Gretchen Silva! You must be hungry, because you never call me unless you ain't ate yet!" Guilty as charged, Gretchen laughed, "Clara, you know me too well. How are you?" "I'm aight, what up with you? Ya man dumped you or something? Cause you call on Clara for two things: food and man trouble." Gretchen closed her eyes to reflect upon the mess she was in: her mother had passed, the last conversation with Jamel, the soon to be expired relationships she had with the other men, Taye Diggs Therapy and the last report from Dr. Phillips. Trying very hard not to sound depressed, she failed when she answered with a sigh, "Well, both and something else. Do you have a space at the Pink Garden?" Clara stopped her playful interrogation and said, "OK, I'm closing at 3:00 today. We are not serving dinner because Isaac and the kids are taking me out for Mother's Day. I'll make you a plate from brunch and we can talk on the patio." " You sound busy Clara. Are you sure you have time for this? I'm sorry, I had forgotten you were married with children now." It was an honest mistake. Clara, who had no children, married Isaac Walters, a father of two, just last year. Gretchen was still painting them into the Clara portrait in her mind. "I'm never too busy to talk to a friend in need. Do not worry about me. I own the Pink Garden, remember? Tricia, the day manager, is coming in to close so that I can go home early. We have a late dinner reservation for 6:00. So, I'll see you in about twenty minutes?" Gretchen choked as she listened to the sound of true compassion speaking to her for the second time in a day. "I love you Clara" is all that she could say with a sniffle and hung up the phone.

Twenty five minutes later, a sky blue BMW Z4 eased into a parking space on the west side of the Pink Garden. It was an exquisite place, which looked like an enormous red cedar pergola style gazebo, which had its center widened to accommodate the restaurant. There were no windows, but the exterior walls were made of clear glass. Pink Garden was transparent, except in the rear where the restrooms, employee area and kitchen were located. Bark and greenery covered every connecting beam and column and pink flowers were everywhere. Gardens and patios dominated about sixty percent of the land around it. Customers could dine in front and on both sides of the building. A pair of black Jimmy Choo lizard print pumps stepped out of the BMW and in them was the always tastefully dressed Gretchen Silva. She wore skinny black Hudson jeans topped off with a flowing floral print blouse by Elie Tahari. Her black leather handbag matched her shoes and her tearful eyes were covered by black Gucci shades. Even when mourning, she made an effort to be presentable and never forget who she was and what she represented. She was Gretchen, strong, independent, successful, and needed no one. Today was different, though she carried the heroine image outwardly; inwardly the martyr was breaking down. Clouds of tears were washing her soul as she took humbling steps towards the East Garden. Clara's table would be located on a secluded patio in the back.

With arms opened wide, Clara greeted her long time friend and classmate since the second grade. She had prepared herself for a serious conversation. Whenever Gretchen had problems with a man, she was either jovial or livid. She would be laughing about the burden she had unloaded or be angry because he was caught cheating before she could tell him that he meant nothing to her. Clara could not recall a time when her friend was not in control or needed help. This time, a depressed and weakened little girl embraced her. After they stood apart, Clara pointed to a dainty brown wrought iron table with two matching chairs. Two covered dishes, two glasses of iced tea, two folded napkins and silverware had been placed casually on the table's glass top. "Have a seat."

"Clara thank you so much for this." Gretchen said just before uncovering her dish and diving into the steamy pasta and vegetables. Simultaneously, Clara uncovered a Green Delight salad and bowed her head to give thanks. She placed a napkin on her lap and began to eat. "Where's the rest of your food?" Gretchen asked. "Oh, I'm saving myself for dinner." Clara laughed. Between bites, they talked about Mother's Day in the Pink Garden. It had been so busy that Clara used her entire staff from the morning and evening shifts. They even added four tables to each garden. Most of the customers were new and did not know that they were losing some of the charm the semi-private areas the gardens would normally give them. Her delivery team barely had time for a real break during the breakfast run. Her staff's hard work had paid off well. They made $5,900 more that time than they had ever before in the same six hour period on other holidays.

Just before finishing brunch, Clara asked Gretchen about her life. "Ok now Grete, tell me what's going on." By this time, Gretchen had collected herself enough to answer and for the first time it was the whole story. She told Clara about missing her mother, the reading of her will and the invisible pole she held between herself and her sisters. Then honestly, she told her that the player life style was getting old and quite tiring. Her affections were torn between her ideal lover and the man who loved her truly. She had taken Jamel's proposal seriously, but feared that she would not be able to bear him children. She began to reconsider adoption, an option she through of before Mama got sick. Dr. Phillips would give her a biopsy and some other tests next Thursday. She feared that uterine cancer would take her fertility just as it had taken her mother's life. Slowly losing control, the shield of self-pity and over-indulgence became too heavy. Gretchen was finally growing enough to face reality and prioritize life. Her only problem was that she did not know where to begin. "I just feel helpless. No hopeless." Clara looked relieved and sighed with a twinkles in her eyes, "Grete, you are on your way to *better days.* Do you know that was the deepest you have gotten with me? You are opening up and sometimes that will hurt, but it is a good hurt. When something destructive is pulled out of your soul, it is like removing a tack, a nail, or even a splinter from your skin. It goes in with pain and it leaves you in pain, but you will heal after they're out." She then smiled and said, "You are neither helpless nor hopeless. God is our ever-present help in time of trouble and that is your hope. He is working in you now. Just look at yourself Grete. It is evident that you love your sisters dearly. If you did not, your distant relationship with them would not be a concern. A few months ago, you wanted to adopt a child and here you are today, wanting to have your own. This whole thing is incredible! My girl is in love and wants to marry her baby's daddy too! "Clara clapped her hands in delight and then raised them to heaven to give thanks.

Gretchen shook her confused head, "I still don't know what to do about all of this" Clara answered simply, "You don't do something about everything. Well, you do, but not all at the same time. You take this one-step and one day at a time. That way resolving these issues doesn't become overwhelming." "One day at a time..." she echoed Clara's words of wisdom. " That's what Mama used to say to us." Clara looked at her seriously and advised, "Grete, you'll know how to handle each of these situations as you face them. I think the best place to start is with your lovers. Those additional relationships are an unnecessary weight." Gretchen interrupted, "I knew you would say that! Clara, you know I do not hold on to men for long. It gets too complicated. Accepting the fact that I date a lot has always been hard for you to understand. So naturally, you would say that first. I know that you are trying to help. Just don't get into judging while you're at it." Clara frowned at the accusation of judging her friend. She had always been honest with her. When Gretchen first told Clara about her men, she told her that dating alone was fine, but adding relations to that could be dangerous in so many ways. Gretchen blew off her advice and said she was not that type of a woman. She told her she wanted to keep her freedom and if she found someone special, she would settle. But that is not what happened. When she found a man who was worthy of a second or third date, he became her beau, exclusively. The relationship usually lasted a few months and he was replaced by a new beau. Three years ago, when Gretchen's mother became ill, she found herself in a relationship with two men. As the illness progressed, so did the number of relationships. During this time, she began to have relations with them. She drew further away from a family who needed her physical presence. Her days at the spa and even her shopping became excuses for not being there. She disguised her getaways as work related activities. Determined never to become trapped by being an involuntary caregiver who is socially and emotionally deprived, Gretchen fortified herself with work and debauchery. She would get all of the attention and love from temporary relationships and move on before she gets her heart broken. Clara was aware of all of this and her only concern was that her friend did not get a disease or end up as the victim of a crime of passion. She had to defend herself from the accusation, "Gretchen you know better than that! The word of God says not to judge or you will be judged. I have not judged you as a woman, but I have the right and responsibility to tell a person that certain activities would harm them. It is like posting a detour sign in front of road that is flooded. We have already talked about how this lifestyle threatens your physical well-being. What about its threat to your soul?"

She wiped her mouth with her napkin and slammed it on the table. "Clara you're not gonna start preaching to me about salvation are you? I got saved at the age of nine." "No, I'm not going to preach, I'm only reminding you that every time you have intercourse with another man, you create a soul tie with him and every woman he had connected with and every man she had connected with and so on. Grete, I am just saying that these relationships may provide you with a mental escape from your problems, but they have taken over your life. I know your schedule. When you are not working, you are running from man to man. It is as if you are trying to fill some void that is constantly leaking what you have put into it. You have a lot of problems. I suggested that you start here, only to give you more thinking time and space. I'm not here to hurt nor judge you."

Gretchen became silent. With trembling hands, she reached into her purse and handed her friend Amelia Covington's card. "I'm calling her tomorrow for an appointment." Clara gave the card back and smiled. Changing the subject, she said, "So, today you will read your mother's will. You are going to read her will, her heart's desire on Mother's Day. Farlinda was right. This is the perfect time and I can feel it in my spirit too."

Chapter IV
Mama's House

4:45 PM

Gretchen parked on the street in front of Mama's house. It was a green Victorian with white trimmings and shutters. A white picket fence enclosed its perfectly manicured lawn. The front door was at the center of the long porch and steps were a few feet out in front. A swing for two and four spider plants hung from its ceiling. Two rocking chairs and an umbrella can were left on the porch from the funeral. Jasmine, Pansies, and Pink Primrose flourished in two flowerbeds on both sides of the steps. She had been there for about ten minutes now, writing her "Dear John" letters to Vaughan, Garrett and Malcolm. Each one was short sweet and read the same way:

Dear _____,

You are a very dear friend and I value our relationship. We both knew that it wouldn't be long term, so I'm telling you the time to end it is now. Serious relationships usually end painfully, that's why I kept it real with you and told you I wasn't ready to commit. Now neither of us has to be hurt. I have enjoyed your company and I'll never forget the time we had together.

During this time of loss, I'm doing a lot of soul searching and I've decided to make some drastic, but necessary changes. The first is to repair my love life. I'll no longer have short-term relationships, because I've found the one man I can commit to.

Again thanks for the good times. I hope you find the woman who complements you too.

Best Wishes,
Gretchen

As she sealed the last envelope, Farlinda parked behind her. Gretchen peered though her rear view mirror to watch her sister fumble around her car. She appeared to be moving objects around. Then very slowly, she peeled herself out and Gretchen stood beside her to assist. "Farlinda you're moving slower than you did when carried Raine and Florin at seven months. Raine came out as an eight-pound wolf. Florin was the big ten-pound bear. So what in the world do you have inside if you now, a baby whale?" Farlinda did not have the energy to slap back, so instead she rolled her eyes and asked, "Why do you have to refer to my children as animals?" "...because they're wild and crazy." She was just about to tell Gretchen about herself, when Gretchen continued to say, "Now really sis, what were you doing in the car? It looked like you were moving something around." Farlinda burst into laughter, "My big body!" Actually, she had crushed the packaging from a burger and fry she had just eaten and forced it into a bag, which had lodged itself deep in the far corner of the floor on the passenger side. Earlier, she had lied to Marshall saying that her sisters were bringing food to Mama's. There was no way of stomaching another nasty meal that day.

She handed Gretchen her five pound crocheted purse and said, "Here, you can carry my little lamb. Now give me a hand so that I can get out of this bug!" Farlinda laughed again when Gretchen's arm dropped from the weight of the purse and almost wet her pants when she struggled to help her get out of the Volkswagen Beetle.

"What in the world do you have inside of this bag?" Gretchen could not imagine what else could a woman need other than her wallet, phone, gum, lipstick and a comb. Farlinda locked her elbows with her sister and went on to explain as they headed towards the sidewalk. She loved their small talk because each time she would give Gretchen glimpses into the busy, yet rewarding world of a working mother. Judging by Gretchen's sighs grunts and grimaces, she thought that her stories turned her off to family life. Actually, she was intrigued and impressed by her. Farlinda answered her question, "Well, let's see... I have my wallet, a pen, a mini note pad, black berry, calculator, brush, my apple & water for snack, prenatal vitamins, dental hygiene kit, panty liner, my make up bag, my brush, hair cream, hand lotion, sanitizer, granola bars for Raine & Florin's snack, baby wipes, lady wipes, a pack of Tic Tacs and three sample bottles of a new fragrance I'll be selling. Want one?" They stopped on the porch in front of the door and Gretchen was visibly sorry for asking Farlinda a personal question.

Shantise beeped her horn, announcing her arrival. Unlocking elbows, her sisters waved. Farlinda opened the door, then she and Gretchen waited for Shantise in the foyer. They observed their baby sister carrying herself as "down" this day. Assuming she was missing her mother, they both hugged her as she came in. Gretchen began to regret being there and asked, "Farlinda, of all the days we could be doing this, why Mother's Day? Why do we have to go through Mother's things today? You should be at home with Marshall and the kids, opening gifts and having some fun" Farlinda would not allow her to back out, "My family has already stuffed me with a home cooked meal and about the gifts, they give me love every day. Besides that, you will not have another free day for two or more weeks. Let's get this over with before you disappear again." Gretchen took no offense to hearing about her own crazy-woman lifestyle, but she was totally revolted to hear how the "queen" had settled for so little on her special day. She lit as she confronted her sister's humility, "You got a home cooked meal and no gift? No way! You mean to tell me the burger boy didn't buy you a Cracker Jack ring, a kiddie meal, a buy one get one free cone, a rose or something?" Shantise coughed out a chuckle in her fist and turned her back on the conversation which had the potential of becoming a feud. Farlinda snapped back, "Gretchen, I'm not as materialistic as you are! Marshall does not have to buy me everything in order for me to know that he loves me. Little things mean a lot and I appreciate anything he places in my hand. On my birthday, he gave me a daisy. Yes, a single daisy and I loved it. It was a corny little gift, but he's saving to give me a vacation after the baby is born."

With that, Gretchen became silent. Her face tensed and she rolled her eyes away from the pathetic, baby bearing, bred winning man-raising fool her majesty had become. If she would have of said those words instead of thought them, she would have lost a sister. Pretending that Farlinda was not there, she calmly asked, "Shantise, tell me that wasn't the whole truth." Shantise could not help it, the giggles poured out upon every other word she said in response, "Grete, it is true! She got a single daisy on her birthday! And I do not believe she ate that stuff the kids and Marshall made for her this morning! It smelled like a wicked blend of cake, fish, rice, and bacon!" That was it! The queen had died before the martyr could. Gretchen, now shocked, appalled and outdone, stopped the fight by surrender, "We did not just have that conversation!" Then shaking her head clean to try to put out her thoughts, she went on to say, "OK, OK, I'll forget it's Mother's Day. I agree with you and let's get this over!" Farlinda was relived to put her personal issues aside and said, "Good were past that now. The sooner we find the will, the sooner we get back to our lives. Shantise, you will be back in your studio. Grete you can go back to the deep voice man in your dreams and I'll go back to my loving family." Shantise saluted the queen "OK Boss Hogg! I mean Daisy Duke." She amused herself with the tired joke and surprisingly Gretchen too. They both laughed as they separated to search for their mother's will.

If it were possible for buildings to marry and have children, Mama's house would have been the child of a library and a country inn. Even though most walls on the first floor were dressed with shelves of books, there was not a single corner that could not be easily touched if necessary. Every chair had a lovely flowered lace blouse, the sofa and love seat had its matching throw. In this very clean and well-organized home, they were certain to find the will soon. Farlinda went to the office and began searching for the file cabinet's key. Gretchen began unsealing the storage bins in the family room and Shantise went to Mama's room to check the dresser drawers.

Upon entering the office, Farlinda had not seen in over a year, she soon learned that Mama had a new hobby. Justine knitted and crocheted blankets, throws, tablecloths and napkins. She had also hand sewed a few rag dolls and the patchwork for quilts. The office formerly swamped by several baskets of yarn and odd pieces of cloth, was now a sewing room. Its appearance was quite professional, as if she had clients visiting. The right side of the room had a large walk in closet, which Mama had rebuilt two years ago to extend from one end of the room to the other. Its three pairs of double doors had gold ribbons tied to its handles serving as unsecured locks. Just outside of the closet was an ironing board, a steamer, a presser and a dress form. A mirror covered the front half wall on the left and a step-height rounded plat form faced it. Office furniture and equipment had taken a small place in the back left half of the room. There was a section for sewing materials. It had a butcher's table in its center and was located on the back wall facing the door. The file cabinet key should have been hidden in some inconspicuous place. Instead, it had been laid on top of a dress pattern that Mama had placed on the very organized butcher's table, which she had used to measure sewing materials. Small pieces of white taffeta, linen, silk and lace were neatly folded on the other side of the table. Strategically positioned on top of a sewing machine, a plastic basket containing spools of white thread, scissors, zippers, measuring tape, some elastic and a pin cushion was found under the table. Three wooden bowls had been stacked inside of the other. They contained a few pearls buttons, hooks & eyes and clear crystal beads. *Mama must've made something very lovely.* Farlinda unlocked the file cabinet and found several receipts, paid loans, and check stubs, which told the story of a woman who made countless sacrifices to raise her daughters well. The will would not be found there, but evidence of love for her girls could be found all over the room. If it was sought after, more of her love could have been unfolded in this place.

Gretchen's bin raiding sent her on an emotional rollercoaster. The first one she opened labeled, "Records" stored an enormous amount of history. She looked at pictures of family members dating back to the early 1900's. Mama had them taped on paper with information about the person photographed below it. She laughed at funny pictures her Aunt Lucy and Uncle Grayson had taken of them at Virginia Beach. One of them was of Farlinda taking a nap and Shantise was about to pour a bucket of sand on her tummy. Gretchen and Henry were giggling and Mama was the tiny woman in the background, rushing from the ocean with her mouth wide open. She cried when she looked at a picture of Henry, taken a week before he died. He was actually hugging Gretchen as she held a tiny fish she had caught. The caption read "Good job Gretchen! Daddy is so proud of you!" "Why didn't you hug me more Daddy?" She said to the picture. That was enough. She closed "Records" and opened, "Thy will be done." The label seemed promising for her purpose. To her chagrin, it was a collection of medical and dental reports on every member of the house hold dating back to when Henry married Justine. There were physician and hospital receipts, discharge papers, and copies of prescriptions. *How boring could this possibly get?* The only thing she found amusing was that the records had been stored chronologically in file folders. Her boredom turned into gratefulness in the records dated after her father's death. The accidents and illnesses had become more serious and it appeared that Mama had handled them differently. These records had Post It papers stuck on the center with prayers of hope and faith written on them. Some of the papers were thanking God for healings. Gretchen would not stop reading these testimonies until Shantise would call her away.

Upon entering Mama's room, Shantise swallowed hard and tears filled her eyes as she scanned the sanctuary.

Her Mamas' faith was remembered there. Echoes and shadows from the past danced through mind. She recalled the last week that she lived in the house with her mother. Shantise's music had become too intense for her mother's ears. They both had become tired of the volume wars, so Shantise waved the white flag by leaving. If she had known of her mother's diagnoses, she would have been more considerate, but Mama spoke nothing about it, until it was too late. The only thing that she did talk about was Shantise needing to have a relationship with the Lord and the rest was yelling about the music. Then Shantise remembered other expressions from The Voice. She looked at Mama's bed and could almost see her mother kneeling and softly calling out her name to heaven. More tears poured down her cheeks and dripped from her face as she recalled the many nights that her mother came to her room when she slept. Sometimes, she was awakened by her presence and overheard the blessing she spoke over her. A gentle kiss was planted on her cheek and the sweet fragrance of Rapture, lingered a few moments after she left. Just then, the scent returned and seemed to have blown in from some place. Following the direction from which it came, she turned from the bed to her window and the curtains billowed. *Strange, the scent of perfume traveling inside a window, how could this be?* There was a chest, she had never seen before, under the window. Before opening the chest, she went to close the window. That did not happen because the window was already closed. Quivering like a frightened child, her heart pounded rapidly. Inhaling shallow puffs of air, she opened the chest that the fragrance had led her to. A large black leather back diary was the only item in the chest. She looked under and behind the chest for the key, with no findings. The curtains blew another puff of Rapture; Shantise fell to her knees and began to scream out her sister's names.

"Farlinda! Gretchen! Get up here quick!" Farlinda was about to untie a ribbon on the closet when she heard her sister's cry. "This better be good news Tise. You know I hate to climb the stairs with this load in my belly." Gretchen had already pulled Shantise from the floor, helped her sit on the bench at the foot of the bed, and was fanning her when Farlinda came in the room. "What happened to Tise?" she asked. "That's what I'd like to know too," Gretchen answered. "The strangest thing happened to me." Shantise began to share. "The scent of Mama's perfume blew towards me from that closed window. I opened that chest and found her diary inside. When I began to look for the key, the curtains moved and I could smell her again! This is weird! I think she's here!" Gretchen was intrigued, but Farlinda felt a bit annoyed that she would run twenty-five extra pounds up a flight of stairs for a ghost story. "Tise, you have always had a strong imagination. Mama's not here and you probably smell yourself." She pulled Shantise's wrist to her nose and sniffed it. "There you go Tise. It is you. You're wearing Rapture!" "No Farlinda! It was not me! Mama smells sweeter when she wears it and you even taught me that. I know the difference between myself and someone else. That was not me. I think this book is some kind of sign or message to us." Shantise was certain of herself and she handed it to Gretchen, who was now seated beside her, "What do you think Grete? Do you think there's something to this?" "Yes, I do. We need to read it," she said feeling the back of the diary as though she was searching for something. Farlinda could not agree, "No, we'll not read it. A dairy is private and we need to respect that." Shantise cut in before she could step on her soapbox of morals, "We will respect her privacy by not telling anyone what we read! Come on Farlinda! We gotta do this!" Gretchen added, "Shantise is right. Mother is gone now and we cannot embarrass her by reading it. If anything at all, we may see what really made her tick beneath all of those 'Praise the Lords' and 'Hallelujahs'. I want to know the real Justine Silva!"

The real Gretchen! Jamel's voice echoed in her mind. *This is not about me! I'm opening this book, with or without her majesty's approval!* Gretchen said to herself, rubbing and poking the backside of the diary until she found a soft spot. Then she picked at the spot, ignoring Farlinda's warnings, "Mama might not like this!" Gretchen, unpeeled a piece of the leather skin, exposing a tiny slice of Velcro which held its' secret compartment secure. There it was tucked inside of the book itself, the key. She handed the book back to Shantise and said, "You found this treasure, now open it." Farlinda twisted her mouth and folded her arms. She sat quietly on her mother's bed, knowing she had lost in this battle of the ethics to her sisters.

Shantise unlocked the diary and began to read, "This diary belongs to Justine Silva. I dedicate the contents of this book to my daughters, Farlinda, Gretchen and Shantise." The war was over and her youngest sister should not have rubbed her victory in her face by teasing. Farlinda snapped back, "It does not say that Shantise! That wasn't funny!" Gretchen looked over Shantise's shoulder to verify the dedication. "Oh my God Farlinda, she's not kidding. It says that on the first page." The older sisters became quiet as Shantise continued to read.

Chapter V

The Bedroom

I hope you don't feel as if you are invading my privacy by reading this diary. So, if you are struggling with a little bit of guilt, let it go. My darling daughters I wrote this diary for you to read when I pass on to Glory. This book is the very special and informal will I wrote for you. Shantise, I believe you would be the one to open the book. You were always the nosiest one. I can count on you to pull your sisters in. You probably had to pull Farlinda a little harder.

Beyond my legal will, I wanted to share some personal thoughts with each of you. Since you were babies, Henry and I taught you about the Lord.

Gretchen interrupted in a tone of boredom, "Here we go again for the one millionth time, another sermon." Farlinda hated disrespect and had to say something back, "Gretchen Lynette Silva, for once, can you listen to Mama's opinion, even if you don't agree with it? I am a Scientologist, but always listen to others views. We call that respect!" Gretchen thought it was time to put the queen in check, "Listening? When did you begin to listen to anyone? You certainly know how to tell everybody what to do. I tried to tell you about that sorry tail Marshall, but you did not listen to me. I told you ten years ago he would not marry you and here you are today with almost three of his kids. You have no certificate, no ring, and not even a Mother's day gift! What happened, are you a born again Scientologist?" Farlinda had no idea from where this kind of hostility was coming from. Gretchen had not only grown tired of her own lifestyle, but watching her sister settle for less was killing her. "That was cold and uncalled for and I didn't deserve it!" Shantise cut in again to stop the banter, "Will you two heathens be quiet and listen to Mama's message?" Farlinda said no more, but took her apple and water out of her purse. Gretchen answered, "Sure, I guess I can hear her final sermon. Read on Shantise."

Since you were babies, Henry and I shared the Lord with you. My heart's desire is that you will know the Lord for yourself and begin to live the abundant life that only He can give. The life I'm talking about isn't the one filled with material things, but things eternal.

I have some stories about women for each of you to ponder. You have heard of them before in the children's church and youth group, but not the way Mama's gonna tell them. Even though they may be a little humorous, please take them seriously.

Farlinda, you, being the oldest would naturally receive my first message. Your sister Gretchen is my workaholic, but you are a woman in overdrive! You run a successful business while raising two children. You have supported Marshall's every failed endeavor and have become the woman of his dreams; one who accepts him fully and give him unconditional love with no red tape to mess things up. You now carry his third child! You have always wanted to marry him, but have denied the very desire of your heart. Your patience has shortened (having three babies will do that to you) and you are ready for some satisfaction in your life. Praise the Lord! Jesus calls that satisfaction-quenched thirst! Now pay close attention to the story about the Woman of Samaria.

During the ministry years of Jesus, He was doing His thing (teaching and healing) in the area of Judea. He had to cut His visit short because the Pharisees heard that He made and baptized more disciples than John (and you know they didn't like that). So, quite naturally, they would want to check Him out. Jesus didn't have time for that foolishness. He had a lot more preaching and teaching to do, so He went to Galilee. On His way, He had to pass through Samaria. He stopped in the city of Sychar. It was near a place that Jacob had given to Joseph. One of the most historic landmarks of the city was there, Jacob's Well. That thing must have been a couple of thousands of years old and people were still using it! Jesus sat by the well to take a break. It was about the sixth hour of the day, which was around noon, when a Samaritan Woman came to draw water. Now this was an unusual time of day to get water because most of the women did it in the morning. I can imagine her approaching the well, looking around and talking to herself.

She would have said, "Good no one is around! I can get my cooking water in peace. Lord, I just get so tired of those gossiping hens pecking at me. High noon is the only break in the day to avoid them." Upon hearing her say "Lord" Jesus gave her his full attention. When she finished, He stood and said, "Are you talking to me?" He had been seated on the other side of the well out of her view, so obviously His appearance startled this poor woman. "What! Who are you and what do you want?" She had prepared herself to give Him all of her shopping money, because now she could see that this stranger was a Jew. You know Jews and Samaritans were enemies and she didn't want any trouble. He knew what she was thinking as He rubbed perspiration off His hot face. Dear Jesus was so tired, thirsty, and not in the mood for some drama. Remember He just left the crazies back in Judea. So He raised His sweet hands and pleaded His innocence, "I am Jesus, a thirsty carpenter from Nazareth. May I have a drink please?" With a whole lot of suspicion, she barked back, "Do you really think I should be giving a strange Jewish man some water?" Though tired, Jesus went on to teach this poor soul a lesson she would never forget. "Miss, if you knew God's gift and knew who is asking you for a drink, you would have asked him for a drink. He would have given you living water. Now she thought He was an idiot. "You don't have a bucket, a dipper, or anything to get the water. Do you know how deep this well is? You can't reach down there with your bare hands and give me water. (He bit his bottom lip, nodded "yes" and raised his brows at the thought of doing that) So, how on God's green earth do you suppose you can give me water." Momentarily, she paused the tongue-lashing. He raised a finger to interject an, answer, but it was too late. She whipped out the answer to her own rhetorical question, "What is it that you're really trying to say? Huh! You must think you're special. Do you think you are more important than Jacob?"

After that, Jesus sat down again. It may take a while to explain this one. He said, "People who drink natural water will become thirsty again, but I'm talking about water that will quench them forever. This water brings up a spring in the spirit that leads to eternal life." This got her all excited and she said, "That's amazing! Give me this water, so that I'll never have to come back here!" (You know she wanted that water really bad. At the same time, she'd avoid seeing the snobs and busybodies even more often.) She lowered her bucket into the well. Jesus smiled and rubbed his brow thoughtfully. It pleased Him to see that this lil snapper had some faith. Then He gave her something to think about and said, "Call your husband and bring him here," She said, "I don't have a husband." Then He let it rip, "It's true you have no husband. You've had five and the man you live with now, is not your husband." She didn't get embarrassed by what He said, but she was surprised that a stranger knew that much about her. "You must be a prophet! (She was impressed, but still tested Him a bit further) Now Mister Prophet, did you know that our ancestors worshipped on this mountain? You Jews say that people must worship in Jerusalem in order to do it properly. Now who is right?" He helped her draw the heavy bucket up and answered, "A time will come when Samaritans will not worship on this mountain or in Jerusalem. God is a spirit, who desires true worship. So everyone who worships Him must do it in spirit and in truth." That made her feel pretty good about herself. She added one more thought before handing him a dipper of water from her bucket, "I do believe that's true and I also believe that the Messiah is coming" He took the dipper from her hand and drank while He could, because He knew that water would have been spilled all over Him after He responded to that. After a big gulp, He smiled and said to her, "I am He, the One and only speaking to you now." With that, she jumped up and ran to tell everybody about this strange man who knew everything about her.

He was right about the water too. It went everywhere!

Farlinda had drifted off into sleep during the part of the story when Jesus asked for a drink. She knew the story well and did not feel guilty for catching forty winks. Her subconscious led her deep into a dream where she would have a heart to heart talk with her mother. "Wake up Farlinda! My story was not meant to put you to sleep. Wake up!" Rubbing her seven and a half month belly, she murmured, "I'm sorry Mama. Sometimes the little one makes me so tired." Farlinda's tight braids immediately felt better when Mama rubbed them and said, "I know he does, but you need to really hear me this time. This is of course my last sermon, according to Gretchen." "I know, I know. My ears are open." Farlinda gave Mama the same blank stare she gave her whenever she "preached" to her and Marshall. "Your ears are always open, but what about your heart? The Samaritan heard Jesus with her heart. Like you, this woman lived with a man to whom she was not married. That never became an issue in their conversation, because she was seeking the right way to worship God." Farlinda gave her mother an inquisitive stare as she asked, "What are you trying to say Mama? You're ok with unmarried cohabitation, but my way of worship isn't good enough?" Mama tried to explain, "Now, wait a minute! Do not get the message all twisted. I am trying to tell you about the heart and the relationship that the Lord wants to have with you and Marshall. Just give me one last moment to share this. Please just listen." Her image began to slightly fade as Farlinda began to unload the frustration she had penned up for so long. She had respected her mother with silence during these talks, but this time the silence broke. "No Mama! You listen to me! My spiritual life is good, my business is prospering, I am in love with my children's father and we are happy. What else could I possibly need? You think I need to have a relationship with Jesus, someone I can't even see?" Mama faded a little more as Farlinda continued to rant, "Really Mama, an invisible man? You do not even believe that is possible yourself! Isn't that what you are so afraid of? You are afraid that if I do not get married, my relationship with Marshall will disappear. Well that's not going to happen!" Mama's image was transparent now. Reality hit Farlinda in the face as if a bucket of iced water was thrown at her. She panicked realizing that she had been arguing with an apparition and had missed the message she tried desperately to deliver. "Mama, wait! Do not go! I'm so..." Before she could finish, Mama interrupted using the weakening power she had left to speak one last time, "Farlinda, I'm not giving up on you. I'm praying for you now, here in this great cloud of witnesses." Her image became a mist and it blew out of her window.

The scent of Rapture awakened Farlinda. She looked at the window with hopes of seeing her mother. There was nothing to be found except a closed window. She rubbed her head and felt the braids, which no longer gave her pain. "Back so soon sleepy head?" Shantise teased her. "You'd better stay awake. She wrote another story for you." "Ok then we'll read it later. Let me see that book. Maybe if I read something I can wake up." Shantise gave her the book and Farlinda began to flip pages until she saw Gretchen's name written on top of one of them. "Hum, now this might be interesting. It's addressed to Gretchen." "Hold on just a sec" Shantise requested a moment to make her body feel more comfortable. She took a pillow from the bed, and lied belly down on the floor. She used it as a chest support and bent her elbows over it. Her face rested in the palms of her hands, "Alright, I'm ready now." Considering Gretchen's lifestyle, Farlinda paused a moment. She had some ideas about the various species of worms she would find in this can she was about to open. Her eyes locked with Gretchen one more time to get her approval. Life was changing for her and she had nothing to lose. "Go ahead Farlinda. Read it."

Gretchen, you remind me of the Queen of Sheba. Having it all—wealth, looks, and brains! The only things you're missing are some good looking male servants.

Gretchen coughed and Farlinda raised her eyebrows. Shantise was still as clueless as her mother seemingly was about Gretchen's men. *Though you appear to have it all together in this world, there is so much more life God wants to give you. I know about your desire to adopt a child and why your health status frightens you so much that you won't. I want you to be fearless, before jumping to any conclusions.*

Farlinda stopped reading to inquire, "What's going on with your health?" Shantise sat upright and stared at her sister in fear, "Are you sick Grete?" Gretchen did not know the answer either. "I don't think so and I'm not worried about my health either. Mother thought she knew everything about everybody. She barely gave me the time of day. How could she possibly know a thing about me? I'm fine, really fine!" Farlinda and Shantise knew better. Childhood was a half- lonely experience for Gretchen, but her mother tried desperately to make up for lost time when she finished high school. She no longer had to work two jobs, Shantise had finally calmed down and Farlinda had a new family. Mama called her often and tried to visit her too, but it was too late. Gretchen did not need her anymore, so she barely gave her mother the time of day. "Grete, you know if something is wrong, Tise and I are here for you. Do not cut us off any more. You're isolated enough and you don't need to go through anything alone." Gretchen gave a smile of confidence and said, "Stop it now. There is no reason to get mushy. I said I am fine. Just read the story, please." Neither of her sisters was convinced that she was "fine." They knew by her fake smile that she was hiding something. Gretchen was a locked safe that could not be cracked. Instead of wasting the effort to make her talk, Farlinda continued to read the diary for further clues.

Gretchen, I want you to hold on to the Lord. Pull on His robe until He gives you your heart's desire. Remember what happened to Jesus on the road to Jairus's house? That's right; I said something happened to Jesus. He didn't do anything except be the son of God and He had an unexpected experience with a woman like you. You know that the life of the body is in the blood. This woman had been bleeding for twelve years! For twelve years, life was seeping through her bandages! You are no different Gretchen. Though you have every possession a woman could possibly want, your soul is dripping life.

Desperation guided this woman as she pushed her way through a thick crowd of confusion. Dozens of people had surrounded Jesus, pleading for His help. Some of them were crying and screaming out: Hosanna! Help me Lord! Heal me please! Son of David, have mercy! I'm blind! Save me! Everybody wanted to touch Him, but not as much as this woman. When she couldn't get close enough to touch His hand, she thought "If I could just touch His cloak, I'll be healed." That's exactly what happened! She sprang as hard as she could toward Him, knocking over a few people too. Her finger tip brushed the hem of his cuff and she felt something warm and wonderful slide all over her body. He demanded, "Silence!" and everybody got quiet. Jesus could barely believe what had happened to Him. Someone was healed and He didn't see that person's face. He felt power flow out of Him to some unknown place. For the first time, Jesus asked a question that He truly did not know the answer to, "Who touched me?" Now the average person in the crowd wanted to answer and say, "I did Lord, when I asked for my healing." But they didn't because he had told them to be silent. Everybody was a little scared at this point. They didn't know if someone had hurt or made Him feel uncomfortable. Then one of His disciples tried to make light of the situation and said, "Actually Lord, they were all touching you..." "Oh no, this was no ordinary touch. Some desperate person just reached out for healing" They all knew that they had, but remained quiet until a woman among them began to weep tears of joy. The voice matched the touch and Jesus went to her and said, "Your faith has made you whole!"

You see Gretchen, that woman's situation could have been easily calculated as hopeless. She could have died in that condition, but she was hopeful. I can imagine how weak she must have been, yet she used all of her strength to press through a crowd. You can do the same thing, trust that God can handle whatever it is that's ailing you. That sick thing that caused you to avoid your family is the root of your illness and your un-rested soul. The sick thing that I'm referring to is something that you gave birth to as the result of pride joining the un-forgiveness. A great *part of your healing will come from forgiveness. When you forgive, you are not only releasing the un-forgiven from their trespasses, but freeing your mind and body from the stress of holding on. You may not believe this but some people see you as "stuffy" and "stuck up." Just the sounds of those words indicate that something is packed and clogged on the inside. People, who are prideful, are often wearing a formidable or superior façade. You have been hurt, therefore: you have covered yourself in the pride of life to protect your broken spirit. Success is sweet, luxury is good, but overindulgence is a red flag. My dear sweet Gretchen, I know that you have paid your dues during childhood and now you are reaping the benefits, but don't forget the most important things are the relationships. I'm not only talking about your relationship with your sisters, but settling down with that one special man that God has for you. Yes baby, I know you have your good share of male servants, but it's time to release them and move on.*

Shantise broke in, "Grete, are you a player?" Gretchen bowed her head in shame. She then looked at and Shantise and answered, "I was, but not anymore." Before resuming reading the diary, Farlinda smiled and said, "The truth shall make you free."

I encourage you Gretchen to press on and touch the hem of your deliverer's garment. He will give you healing, peace and stability. If you allow Him, He'll make His home in you. The word "home," brings me to my next story. It's about a house that wasn't a home for a woman named Hannah.

Baby you know that too many men can be quite a burden for one woman to manage, so the opposite must be a neurotic nightmare. I can just imagine the headaches Elkanah may have suffered from the cat fights between his two wives. The problem they had with each other was the same sick thing you have living in your heart. You see, Peninnah had children and she constantly flaunted the treasures of her fertility before the barren Hannah. The pride didn't come from possessing the treasures, but it was the breastplate for her jealous heart. Knowing that Elkanah actually loved Hannah "killed" Peninnah daily. On the other hand, Hannah had to deal with bitterness. Forgiving a spiteful haughty woman wouldn't be an easy task, but not impossible.

Can you imagine how these women must have sounded? How they looked? How they behaved? When you read about them, give Peninnah a deep preacher woman's voice. She's very pretty with dark Egyptian features. Her clothing is made of fine purple linen with a matching veil. Wealth displayed itself in her jewelry, especially the golden moon earrings. Onyx beads were sewn on the surfaces of her goat hair necklaces, bracelets and anklets. Every piece of jewelry tinkled as the golden charms, which were sewn at the ends, tapped upon each movement she made. During this time, she wore makeshift footwear, because her feet were too swollen for sandals. Peninnah's feet and ankles were wrapped in sheepskin and the base was a bed of soft wool. She secured the" boots" with long leather straps, which were laced from the bases to the shins. In the public's eye, she was a pitiful pregnant lady, but at home an instigator of endless arguments.

Hannah's voice was as soft and delicate as her tiny Hebrew body. She had a cute baby face and the prettiest eyes in town. Even though she was about the same age as her adversary, people had often mistaken Hannah as Peninnah and Elkanah's grown daughter. Hannah wore a white linen dress covered with a dark blue woolen tunic. The veil worn on her beautiful black hair matched it in color, representing her sorrow for barrenness. A braided belt, never tied tightly hung loosely around her waist. She believed that tightness would impair her chances of one day becoming fertile. Unlike the very pregnant Peninnah, Hannah didn't have to concern herself with swollen feet. She could wear any of her four pair of sandals on any day. That was just another reason for Peninnah to hate her. Hannah used every quality and luxury she was envied for possessing as weapons during their quarrels.

I can see the two of them about to heat up a nasty spat. It would occur in the evening just before supper when the laundry had dried. Hannah would be the one to carry the basket back to the log where she and Peninnah sat to fold the blankets and garments. Peninnah would start by taunting, "Well sister Hannah, it's about that time to get our portions from Elkanah. I'm looking forward to getting a great portion. It should be a lot bigger than yours. He and I have lots of children to bless and I'm certain to get *something extra for giving him something extra." She grinned at Hannah and said, "You know what I'm talking about girl." She rubbed her belly, licked her lips and bit her bottom lip as if she had tasted something delicious. Then she sighed and rolled her eyes, as she reminisced on moments with her man. She shot them back at Hannah to see if she had noticed her daydreaming and of course she did. This time Hannah tried not to allow herself to be provoked into arguing so quickly. Her reply was short and sensible, "I may not have any children, but I expect a big portion too. Elkanah loves me and I'll get the same blessing as you." Without even trying, she had slapped her back by using the "L" word. The fight was on! Round One had ended with minor injuries from the insults.*

Round Two- Peninnah turned sideways to face her and boast a bit more, "Elkanah loves me" she imitated in Hannah's girlish voice. "If he loves you so much, why is it that he spends more time on my side of the house?" With that, she sucked her teeth as her rolling eyes guided the position of her body away from her opponent. Then Hannah cocked her head to the side to size up the green-eyed monster and jabbed back, "It's not love that drags him to you. It's your noisy, untamed little crumb snatchers that he's always running to discipline. He's just visiting to put some order in your space. Elkanah is a man of peace and sanity. I wonder where the children get their madness." She rubbed her right temporal and gazed thoughtfully into Peninnah's eyes for a clue to this "mystery." The jabs hurt, but there was no stumbling. It was possible that these women could do this until nightfall.

Round Three-Penninah had used the best of her catty banter to slap and jab at Hannah. This time she was certain to leave some deep bite marks from brutal mocking and dark sarcasm. The drama began by grabbing Hannah's arm and demanding help for her fake labor. With her, other hand she cupped the lower part of her belly and moaned, "Oh! Oh! I feel another blessing coming now! Quick! Grab some towels! You know what to do! Come on Hannah it's time!" She released her belly and pointed her finger toward the east corner of the house, the area they had been using for birthing and nursing Peninnah's other children. Hannah dropped the scarf she had been folding to help the Oscar deserving actress rise from the log. As she stood, Peninnah bent forward. Her shoulders bounced as she released a choppy laugh. At that moment, Hannah knew that she'd been toasted and as Shantise would say, "She got punked!" No longer able to have a clean fight, Hannah took off the gloves and screamed, "You.....! You....! Pregnant proud heifer! I hope your baby looks like the ugly animal its mother is! Aw! I can't stand you Peninnah! You're so evil and hateful!" That made her laugh and tease more, "Stop hating and help me deliver this child!" Hannah kicked the laundry basket over and stormed away. After taking a few steps, she turned around to give her the last piece of her mind. She pointed at Peninnah's belly and declared, "After this child is born, the next time someone delivers a baby, *you will deliver mine!" Then Peninnah spat out her final insult in her finest preacher woman voice, "Yeah, he'll be just like his mama, a real prophet. Prophesy it girl! Your man-child is coming! Hallelujah!" She began to taunt her mercilessly with a shouting dance as if she was filled with the Spirit. The last blow was a knockout. Hannah felt as though she had fallen to the ground and Peninnah was dragging her body to the edge if a cliff to dispose it. That blow had taken the most precious thing away from Hannah: her hope.*

Hannah's anger turned to sadness as she walked away. There was nothing she could do to help herself, but she knew that her God could. Her feet led her to the temple. She cried bitterly, petitioning the Lord to see her affliction and give her a son. Hannah vowed that if He did, she would give him to the Lord for his whole life. Gretchen, the Lord gave Hannah that baby boy and she kept her promise to Him too. Her son, Samuel, was raised in the house of Eli the priest and he grew up as a great prophet. Now my daughter, I'm asking what are you willing to give to the king in exchange for your healing and peace of mind? I could give you a list of things, but I won't. Instead, I'll tell you where to start and that is: Put your hope in God, your healer and deliverer.

Farlinda stopped reading and put a pen on the page. She noticed Gretchen wiping a few tears and decided to take break. Shantise stood and walked towards Gretchen with a tissue in her hand. The room was still and nearly silent except for the sounds of sniffles. "OK, Mother, I get it" Gretchen whispered. With a weak smile, she reached for the diary, "May I see that please. I would like to read some of Mother's last sermon." "Not yet!" the queen interjected, "I need to get something to eat first!" Farlinda slid off the bed and headed towards the door. "Are you coming?" Shantise and Gretchen shrugged their shoulders and followed the leader downstairs.

Chapter VI

The Kitchen

Farlinda went to the refrigerator and grabbed three canned drinks from the funeral repast. Gretchen took the Diet Coke and Shantise took the Sprite. That left Farlinda with the lemonade. Between the three of them, they created a meal of unsalted crackers, potted meat and fruit cocktail for the hungry monarch. Upon their seating, Gretchen opened the diary and pulled the pen from the page that Farlinda had saved. Flipping the page once, she saw that Mama had finished the Gretchen section. "Hum, it appears that you read the last message for me. The next page says 'Shantise'" The star smiled at the sound of her name hitting the air. Her legs were a large pretzel seated on the chair with her elbows on the table and hands cupping the Sprite. Gretchen sat up tall and erect. She had crossed her legs at the knees and held the book as if she was going to read to a group of school children. Farlinda leaned back comfortably on a padded chair. A few crackers had been spread with potted meat and she worked carefully to make a few more for story time. Gretchen began reading.

Now Farlinda, the Lord gave me a message of love for you, Gretchen a message of hope and Shantise faith...

A very confused Farlinda interrupted, "Wait a minute! She wrote a message to me about love? I thought it was all about worship." A bit irritated, Shantise responded, "You wouldn't know if she did or didn't. Remember, you fell asleep. When you woke up, you wouldn't let me finish reading your part!" Gretchen had had enough of Farlinda's continuously changing attitude towards the diary. She shook her head and said, "Farlinda you are one indecisive sister! At first, you said do not read the diary. Then you tried to convince me to 'listen' to others opinion, which you rarely do yourself. Then you tell Shantise to stop reading the sermon addressed to you and now you are stopping me because you want to go back to the same sermon. My God your highness, what do you want?" Farlinda defended herself, "Grete you know that Mama was one of those stuffy, legalistic church women who always had to do things the "Christian way." She wrote about the Samaritan without judging her or me. Now, that is amazing! My mother, our mother, Justine Silva has written something to me about love! She is not pushing the whole marriage issue again. I think Mama finally got it. What Marshall and I have is about love not a piece of paper!" With that, warm tears flowed over her flushed cheeks. These tears were filled with relief and grief: relieved that Mama and Marshall had "agreed" and grieved because she had lost an ally in her silent war for marriage. Relief and grief turned around in her soul as wrecking ball and roller: destroying dreams and paving the road of frustration and dissatisfaction. Farlinda was drowning in denial and made light of it with a fake smile.

Guilt, shame and sorrow turned Gretchen's body away from her sisters. She dashed into the living room to get tissues. Having full knowledge of Farlinda hopes for marriage she regretted saying that she knew ten years ago that Marshall would not marry her sister. Gretchen was ashamed of herself for leading such a wild life style and criticizing her sister's at the same time. "Damn! At least she tried to do right!" As she returned to the kitchen, Farlinda continued crying and begged an unintelligent but emotional plea, "Gretchen let's read about the love. You know I love, love. I just want the love." A sorrowful Gretchen handed her a tissue, nodded 'yes' and hugged her tightly (for the first time in several years).

Exhausted by Farlinda's Drama Queen Speech on Love, Shantise pleaded for her share of attention, "From 8:15 this morning, you have been demanding something of us. You asked us to find the will. We are here. Then Grete said you are indecisive about reading the diary and she was right! You wanted to eat. We are eating and now!" She shook a potted meat cracker towards her tensed lips. Shantise stopped the rebuke and calmed herself. "Can we hear about the love later? I really want to hear what Mama said to me. Well, at least that way you can get yourself together before we read something heavy and you know the subject of love carries a lot of weight" pointing to Farlinda's belly. They all laughed in agreement. Farlinda dried her eyes with the tissue and said, "I'm ok now Grete. You go ahead and read Shantise's story. The star beamed at the sound of her name.

Shantise you have the faith to move a mountain! You believe you can do anything and be anyone you want to be! Just do not forget who is the author and finisher of your faith. You say things like, "I can do all things through Christ who strengthens me" and many other scriptures that you have learned. I fear that you have become like many Christians. You trust God for the benefits, but you never take the time to truly know Him. Do you remember last year when I taught about Relationships in the young adults Bible class? It was the lesson about how well family members know each other and how well we know the Lord. I read Matthew 7:21 when Jesus said, "Not everyone who says to me 'Lord, Lord!' will enter the kingdom of heaven, but only the person who does what my Father in heaven wants. Many will say to him, 'Lord, Lord! Didn't we prophesy in your name, cast out demons, and do miracles by the power and authority in your name?' Then He will say to them publicly, I have never known you. Leave me you who practice iniquity!" You see God' gifts are given to the unrepentant ones also.

There are two stories about faith and relationship that I must share with you. The first is about a woman who was married to a man who knew, loved and trusted God with all of his heart. This woman did not have the same kind of relationship with the Lord as her husband. As she observed God move in her husband's life, her own faith in God grew.

Back in those days, Abraham and Sarah were known as Abram and Sarai. You see, God had not commissioned them yet. Now the Bible doesn't say that Sarai was with her husband for this little talk with God, but to make a point about faith, I'm adding her.

Just imagine this ancient couple scaling a great hill ever so slowly. Old Abram would encourage his bride to moving onward and upward, "Come on old girl! You can make it! Just two more steps!" A proud wide smile stretches across his wrinkled face, "Ste--------p! Ste---------p! You made it!" Carefully, Sarai straightens her back and rubs it. Exhaling a great breath she brags, "Woo! I made it! I made it!" Abram patted her shoulder, "I knew you could do it! After all of that mumbling and grumbling, you did it!" Sarai laughed at herself because she had complained every step of the way. She bellyached about the rocks, the grass, the holes, her feet, her knees, her back, the this, the that, the everything! Holding a tight grip on Abram's sleeve, Sarai panted, "Now, Abe, what's the big surprise?" He looked at her pensively, wondering if she could bear what would happen next after such a strenuous walk. "The Lord's got another promise for us. Now, let's sit down and listen." Sarai nearly choked upon his words, "Sit? Sit down? Now if I sit down and you sit down... Who's gonna help us both get up? That doesn't sound like good idea!" She cupped her hands above her brow and began scanning the area below, "I and don't see any servants for miles!" Abram chuckled at the apprehension and answered reassuringly, "Sarai, my sweet, have faith. The Lord brought us up this mountainous hill and He'll bring us down, therefore; we will sit and He will raise us. Have faith. "Faith" she echoed thoughtfully. "OK, Faith. We have walked here in faith and now we're sitting in faith." She was still holding his sleeve as she slowly bent her sore knees. With caution, she stretched her other hand below her buttocks towards a large stone she was aiming to sit upon. Abram grabbed the arm of her out stretched hand and assisted in lowering her body safely. Sarai groaned all the way down her carefully measured descent and burst into laughter as she touched the stone. Abram didn't laugh because he had to think quickly about how he would get down there too. To minimize the chances of getting an injury, he didn't straighten his back as he used to in his younger days. Instead, he took advantage of the bent position he held to assist Sarai and continued to slowly squat for his seat. Within a safe inch of sitting, all of a sudden, the Lord spoke in His thundering voice, "AAAAAAABRAM!"

Abram's ninety nine year old bag of bones shook with fear! He fell to the ground. Sarai clung to him the same way you did to me when you were two years old and the drums in the parade frightened you. The concerned Father inquired compassionately, "SON, ARE YOU OK?" Abram rubbed his chest and answered, "Yeah, yeah, Yes Lord, I'm fine." He stammered, "I wasn't ready for your heavy bass voice. It, it startled me." The Lord chuckled, "ALRIGHT SON, I'LL RELEASE THE BASS." He cleared his throat to make the adjustment. With a tone and volume perfected to suit His children, He asked, "How is this one?" Relieved, Abram said, "Ah......, easy" "I'll name this voice the John O' Hurley and the deep bass one the James Earl Jones" The three of them laughed. Abram and Sarai thought that *naming voices was cute, but the Lord had plans for those special sounds. Remember He knew us before the foundation of the earth. He continued in the captivating entertainer's voice, "Abram, I called you here to give you THIS! Now, Stand!"*

Without a thought or groan, Abram and Sarai rose! "Ah!" Abram shouted, "We're standing! You see Sarai! Faith!" The Lord continued as a game show host would to describe the prizes a contestant has won, "Look to the north, south, east and west of where you are. All the land that you see, I am giving to you and your descendants forever." Dear old Abram squinted his eyes and looked in all directions. "I will give you as many descendants as the dust of the earth. If anyone could count the dust of the earth, then he could also count your descendants. Now G_" The Lord was trying to say "Go" but Sarai interrupted and said, "Abe! Here put on your glasses! You gotta see what the Lord is giving you!"

The sisters stopped to laugh at Mama's "Flava." Shantise said "Mama was so crazy. Did people even wear glasses back then?" Gretchen smiled and said, "No. Eyeglasses were invented by Salvino D' Armate around 1283." "Twelve eighty-four" the queen corrected. "Say what?" Gretchen snapped playfully. "You mean you actually paid attention in that Ancient History Class. After all of this time I thought the only thing you got out of it was Marshall's phone number." Farlinda sang back, "Well at least it wasn't Professor Washington's number." An embarrassed Gretchen waved her invisible sword and said "Touché" Disgusted, Shantise shrieked, "Eeeeeew! Grete! Wasn't he as old as Daddy was? Oh my God, that's so nasty!" Shantise tightly closed her eyes and waved her hands beside her ears, motioning "stop" She continued, "Look I don't want to know anything else about your men. Today I learned that you were a player and now that you were Professor's Washington's hoochie! Not only was he old, but he was married with kids and grandkids! This is too much!" Shantise dropped her head on her crossed arms she had just collapsed upon the table. "Grete, Farlinda, the only thing I want to hear is the rest of this story. No more trashy tales from the crypt and the creeper, Ok?" Visibly embarrassed, Gretchen's voice trembled as she carefully explained, "Tise that was my past. I made a lot of mistakes back then. You would never understand how lonely and needy for attention I was. Just today, I decided to get help on dealing with the mess inside of me." She pointed to her heart and made a bitter expression upon the words, "mess inside of me" "I'm not so proud of myself and there's a lot of emotional garbage to clean up. This may take a while, so please be patient. I'm trying to change." Farlinda nodded, "Don't worry about it Grete. The past is behind you and tomorrow will be better. Go back to the story. It was beginning to sound like something great was about to happen." Gretchen let out quick nervous chuckle while exhaling and shook her head at the thought returning to the "sermon." Having another slap of reality, it seemed almost ridiculous at this point to read some half-fictional story about a couple who had been dead for thousands of years. Not wanting to appear as indecisive as Farlinda, she began to read again.

...but Sarai interrupted and said, "Abe! Here put on your glasses! You gotta see what the Lord is giving you!" The Lord was delighted and amused by her enthusiasm, because Sarai had always been the opposite. "Thank you Sarai. May I finish now?" Embarrassed she squeaked back, "Yes Lord. I'm sorry." Then Old Father Abraham put on the glasses and his eyes grew as big as them CD's I bought for your birthday! The Lord cleared his throat and went on to say, "As I was saying, GO! Walk back and forth across the entire land because I will give it to you." Abram's excitement sent a quake throughout his bony frame! You could hear his knees knocking! Sounded like the high notes on a xylophone! "For Me! WooooWeeeee! Come on Sarai, let's walk!" Then they started walking. They even had their servants to do some walking for them!

Well Shantise you know the rest. Abram and Sarai's names were changed by God to Abraham and Sarah because they would be the father and mother of many nations. At the ages of ninety-nine and ninety, they laughed when the Lord said that they would have a son. They thought that the work was done with the birth of their son Ishmael. Sarah had arranged for her maid, Hagar, to marry her husband in order to have a baby for them. I guess you could say they used her as a surrogate mother. Nope, it wasn't over yet! God told Abraham His plans for both of his sons and my goodness, they were great!

I envision Abraham, his wives, and son living peacefully as a family until Sarah became pregnant. You can imagine the tension building as Sarah's belly grew. Abraham must have worried sleepless nights about how he would some someday pass his inheritance onto his second son. The first son was normally the one who would get it, but now what would he do? God said He would make a covenant with Isaac. How could he break this tradition and still bless the first-born? Sarah must have worried that Abraham would pass the inheritance on to her servant's son, because he was the first born. Perhaps he would cleave to his younger wife and prefer her. The covenant and the relationship would be forgotten and Sarah would be treated as an old servant. Hagar and Ishmael had the most to fear. They probably didn't know all about the Isaac's covenant and Ishmael's blessing yet. What they did know is that they were different and that old couple was pretty excited about having a baby.

When Isaac was about a year old, Sarah weaned him. Nursing a baby at ninety-one years of age, must have been a real chore, because she threw him a party to mark the occasion! I guess it was like a big ole birthday bash and everybody was there! (Well actually, his daddy gave him a feast and it was a major event. You get the idea). This is when Ishmael's whole world changed. His Mama Sarah saw him mocking Isaac during dinner and she didn't like it. Not a bit! She had been thinking long and hard about her son's future and that one little act of jealousy tipped the judgment scale to favor Isaac. It was as though the boys were pieces of marble on a balance and Isaac's portion had been slightly heavier. Then the mocking, forced her to release a fifty-pound chunk of marble onto her natural son's side. You know that poor old Abraham didn't sleep that night, because Sarah told him something that left his heart sore. She told him to put out Hagar and Ishmael and that the boys would NOT share an inheritance She had put her foot down! This was when Abe knew how things would pan out between his sons: one would go, the other would stay and space and time would cause them to forget the other. Tomorrow morning the separation would begin.

An hour after dawn broke; the house of Abraham had bathed and dressed for the day. Sarah left her precious baby sleeping on his mat and went out for a short walk with a servant. This would allow Abraham just enough time to tell Hagar to leave. Sarah's emotions had changed from resentment to sadness in the few hours that she did sleep. At this moment, she had reached another level in faith. She had had a baby, put away her suspicions about Abraham's marital preference, and now she was certain what the future would hold for the boys. You know all virtue is birthed out of adversity: pressure brings patience, exposure brings humility, and trials bring faith. Certainly, she was ready to move on to a new day.

Upon her return, Sarah, witnessed the sweetest display of affection. Her heart skipped a beat at the tender sight she beheld. Ishmael and Isaac were seated together on the rug in the gathering space, having breakfast. Isaac's brother had cleaned him, dressed him, and was now feeding him. Sarah touched her heart as she listened to the one-way conversation they shared. "Here you go buddy, your first breakfast as a BIG boy!" Ishmael proudly watched the baby eat from the spoon he'd just filled with porridge and whey. Without a sound, she drew a little closer.

"Ishmael, bring me your brother. I need to tell you a story." Sarah said with her heart full. He rose, handed her the baby, and then sat on a stump beside her. With a deep breath, she began, "Many years ago there was an old man and his wife. They had no children. One day, God promised them that they would have so many children, that they could not be counted. The old woman could hardly believe that she would have children, so she decided to help God. She told her maid to have a child for her. Her maid was an obedient woman and she did as she was told." Ishmael looked pensively at her and said, "Mama Sarah, you're talking about me and mother, aren't you?" She rested her free hand upon his shoulder and said, "Yes, son I am. Well, I see you know the story and now it's time for you to begin to walk into your blessings. What I am saying is, it's time for you to go" Shocked and horrified, he stood and reasoned, "No Mama. We are a family. Families stay together." "No" she whispered back, "This can't work." Ishmael shook his head in sorrow, "No, No Mama! It's all my fault. I should NOT have made fun of Isaac at his feast." He looked into his brother's eyes, missing him already, he began to weep. "Ishmael, listen, the Lord has promised an everlasting covenant with Isaac and to you a great nation. We can't have the both of you in the same land, fighting over who will be the greatest." " Yes, we can Mama! We can live together. I'll change. I am changed. Mama, I'm sorry for hurting you." Tears began to fall and she hugged him in one arm and held his brother with the other. "Son, I have learned to trust God, especially for things that I do not understand. Now you must trust Him too. With faith, you can move a mountain!"

A second after that, Hagar stood at her son's side. She was carrying a sack full of their belongings, a small food bag, and a corked bottle. Carefully she placed them on the ground, then wedged herself between Sarah and Ishmael to hug him. Mocking the words she had just overheard, she sucked her teeth and said, "Well, Mama Sarah pray for my faith. Abraham just gave me a bag of bread and one, ONE bottle of water to take on our journey. I guess this is how the single mother survives, on this little bit and faith. I just hope we don't die out there!" Sarah tried to console her, "Hagar, don't look at what man has given you. God had given you His word, the bread of life! If He can bring life out a dead womb, He can keep His word to you." Hagar just nodded and pulled Ishmael away from Sarah. As they walked away, warm tears washed over his *cheeks and he sobbed silently. His mother bit her bottom lip and tightly held her mouth together to hold the weeping inside. Sarah felt a gentle tug on her shoulder. It was Abraham beckoning her to return to the rug. She could not stop looking at them. Then suddenly she called out, "Ishmael! Ishmael! God has promised to make you a great nation with twelve princes! Hold your head up son and walk into your destiny!"*

Shantise, I want you to always remember to keep the faith, but do it the way God tells you. Learn from Sarah that you do not need to help God by finding quick solutions or taking the first offer someone makes you. Be wise in how you manage your relationships, even with your most trusted friends. To be specific, I'm talking about the trip to Hollywood you are planning to take to with TJ and Velvet.

"How did she know about that?" Shantise interrupted. Gretchen only glanced at her with a "Mama knows" expression and continued:

I don't feel so good about that crew. They look like the kind of kids who will do anything to be famous, even sell their own souls. In TJ's sight, you are just another commodity. You might as well be one of those DVD's he's always carrying around. That Velvet is just as bad. She does not care what happens to her! But I know that your values are different. I know about your love for Christian rap and also that you talked with Mick Chavis of Christian Records about a contract. Why haven't you pursued this any further? Has God called you to rap for Him? Believe me when I say, 'Mick will be calling you'. Pray and see what God has in store for you.

Gretchen closed the diary and sighed, "We'll I guess we all have something to pray about: Mother's last sermon, my goodness." Farlinda jumped off her seat as though it was burning her. "No, not yet! I've got to see what else she had to say to me!" She grabbed the diary and dashed into the living room. After finding her page, she collapsed on the sofa and began to read the passage about love. Her sisters dragged in the room behind the dictator.

Chapter VII

The Living Room

Farlinda, the Samaritan Woman at the well knew that God wanted to give her people much more than they already had. Besides a piece of land and Jacob's Well, the Samaritans were waiting for the Messiah too. She knew that the Messiah would bring clarity to the issue of where should a Samaritan worship God.

She believed the Messiah would help them on every religious issue, but she didn't know how personal He would be until she met Him. You see Jesus told her that God desires true worship. He wants us to be with Him, in His presence. It doesn't matter if we are on a mountain, in the Holy City of Jerusalem, in a church building or behind the counter of Farlinda's Fragrances, God wants our hearts.

Jesus spoke to the woman's heart when He told her all about herself. Without throwing one stone at her, he offered her living water: the water that quenches the thirst for righteousness, which every soul desires. Many people, such as yourself, have tried to satisfy themselves with everything this world has to offer, including the practice of something I call "Me-ism." You know what I mean by that! Too many of us replace an all powerful, all knowing and all ways present God with ourselves. We depend upon theories, compromises, and control to understand our purpose and manage our lives.

Farlinda, I know that you desire to be what Scientologists call a "thetan" and I don't blame you for that. Who wouldn't want to reach her highest potential? In my speculation, a thetan sounds like a god. Did you know that it is written two places in the Bible that we are gods? Understand that we are gods because we are created in His image. Our purpose is to be a reflection of our Father who is in Heaven. Now I guess you wonder what does all of this have to do with the heart. Believe me my daughter; it has everything to do with it. Farlinda, you have a big heart and honestly, I can't think of a person that you haven't shown love to in one way or another. Shantise has a place to nurture her dream because of you and Gretchen has an angel to call her every Sunday morning, just to see if she still has a pulse. Raine and Florin's mother has more patience than I ever did and that Marshall's got it made! I won't talk about your grown child right now, this is about you. You operate in love as a princess, but there's more. Love is fearless and certain. It brings order and completion to all things. Love isn't cynical, it hopes and trusts. Love delivers itself as an item of choice not control. Sometime in the near future, I would like to look down on the Queen of Hearts, operating on this level of love. What I am talking about is a covenant God wants to have with you and if he's willing Marshall too. You see God is love, perfect love. I want to share a story with you about a woman who did not accept God's perfect love because she thought she could find it all in herself. Please my daughter; do not make the same mistake as Mother Eve.

Farlinda straightened her back until it make a cracking noise. Gretchen and Shantise's eyes grew wide in amazement at the sound. "Y'all know what that means?

Farlinda is too old to be having another baby! Girl, you'd better call it quits after this one. Either tie those tubes or tell Marshall to leave you alone!" Gretchen tapped the table as her unofficial gavel, closing the case of Reproduction vs. Common Sense. Wincing her eyes, Farlinda spoke sharply through pursed lips, "No, it means, I'm uncomfortable on this sofa! I need something softer." Without a thought, she snatched a small pillow from beneath Shantise's arm and used it to support her belly. "You're welcome, Your Majesty!" Shantise snapped at her.

Turning the page, Farlinda raised her brow at what Mama had done to it. She had given this story a formal heading, dedicated to "Farlinda, the Queen of Hearts" titled "Eve rejects true Love"

During the day hours, they ate, drank and breathed it. Unblemished bare feet walked upon it and when the night came, they nestled within it. The "it" was love. Love fed them and quenched their thirst. It filled their lungs with life. It covered their feet as shoes and bodies as garments. As the earth became quiet and dark, it wrapped around them as blankets. They were created by Love, they existed in Love and they were in Love.

A thousand years for us, is a day for the Lord. For all of their days, they had what our world today only dreams of: complete satisfaction, needing nothing. Created in the image of God, Adam owned everything. He named every creature including the loveliest, of all, his wife. Adam was the keeper of the garden and when something needed care, he laid his tender hands upon it and watched the renewing begin. He spoke to the flowers to refresh them and sweetened the waters with a song. Effortlessly, he managed the earth's crown and glory.

These living souls resided in the bodies of twenty year olds: eternally young, beautiful, and active. Their senses exceeded the most keen of creatures. Whatever things that they could not see beyond horizons, they could hear or smell them. They could outrun the cheetah, out climb the monkey, out swim the dolphin and outwit the serpent. They challenged each other and played games as children. Eve, the faster swimmer, would often let Adam win the races. It nearly killed him when he lost and she dreaded the thought of perhaps becoming a twenty-year-old widow. In hide and seek, he frustrated her! It would take hours for her find the master of body camouflage. Adam's skin appeared as ferns and moss on trees. He blended amongst the flowers, but the most inconspicuous places were the rivers and the earth itself. Eve and her husband invented dozens of games to play after tending the garden. "Catch the orange," the simplest of them all, was their favorite pastime.

One warm misty morning, they awoke in a playful mood, almost foolish. Adam said, "Get up Second Place and let's have lil fun." Eve laughed at her new name and quipped one back at him, "Yeah, that's right, I am second place! I'm second place to nothing, which makes me number one and you, nothing!" With that, Adam jumped off his bed of leaves and grabbed the orange they'd played with the day before. "Alright Mrs. Smarty No-Pants, it's on now! I challenge you to a new game of catch. I'm calling this one Garden Stretch. Listen carefully to the rules because I'll say them only once. You may throw this orange no slower than forty kilometers per hour. The minimum distance it can be thrown is one half of a kilometer and the maximum is the length of the garden. You cannot stretch your arms beyond five meters to catch the orange. If it flies beyond your reach, you'll have to run to get catch it. Finally, the loser has to pick, prepare and serve breakfast to the winner. Ready?" No!' she yelled. "I can't stretch my arm out five meters, not even one! I can only reach the length of my arm!" Adam laughed at her ignorance. "You haven't tried yet. Now Go!"

In a flash, Eve ran back a kilometer and waited for Adam to throw. When he saw her stop, he sent the orange zooming towards her. Just under forty Kilos per hour it landed "Quash!" in the palms of her hands! Adam fell to the ground and burst out in laughter to the extent of shedding tears. "You fooled me Adam! My hands are a mess! I don't want to play Garden Stretch anymore!" She stormed off to the Euphrates to wash her hands. Realizing his joke wasn't so cute, he ran behind to help. He met her with a handful of wild flowers and whispered an apology, "Sorry, Second to Nothing." Eve, now feeling serene, used her free hand to hold Adam's and led him into the fruit orchard." Let's have some breakfast. I'll pick and you prepare." He nodded and followed.

They agreed to have a three fruit salad, something juicy and crunchy. Eve selected peaches and tangerines for the juicy part. She thought about apples for the crunchy part, then changed her mind and began searching for a suitable replacement. Adam turned south to find something and she walked northward. Eve caught the Tree of the Knowledge of Good and Evil in the corner of her eye and turned to behold its glory.

Its tiny green berries glistened as emeralds in the sunbeams, which had just begun to pierce through the morning mist. She cut her eyes from this and said, "Crunchy not forbidden." Then a sweet voice responded to her, "That's right, it's crunchy, but not forbidden." Eve answered "No, no that's not what I meant and you, whoever you are, know what I meant." The cutest yellow serpent emerged from a branch and smiled at her. "No, my dear Mother Eve. The fruit of this tree is delicious, crunchy and certainly not forbidden. Did the Lord say you shall not eat of this tree?" Startled at these words, she could only shake her head, "yes." He went on, "He said you would die, didn't He?" She whispered, "Yes." The serpent giggled and teased, "You foolish girl, perhaps seeing is the only way to make you believe." He picked a berry and began to eat it. Eve gasped. Savoring each chomp, he moaned in delight, "Um, this is so good: crunchy, juicy and it tastes divine. Oh, Eve this is the perfect fruit." Upon his third bite, he coughed and shook violently. "What's wrong with you?" "I'm dying! I'm dying! Help me Eve!" His eyes rolled back into his head, he lied still and appeared lifeless. "Are you dead?" she screamed, "Answer serpent! Are you dead?"

Serpent opened his eyes and laughed uncontrollably. Eve had been tricked twice in a day. Adam hearing the screaming and laughing from a distance, turned back to investigate. When he arrived, he froze at the sight of all the strange things that were happening. His Eve having the appearance of being under a spell was conversing with a serpent. Then sweetly, another voice spoke to her. It came from the Tree of Life, "Choose me Eve. I am Life. I am Love. I am all that you need." She turned toward the voice which came from the tree only a few meters behind Adam and looked at it as if it was the first time she had seen it. Her bewildered husband: invisible. "You will not die if you eat of this tree! But your eyes will be opened and you shall be as gods, knowing good and evil." Now facing Serpent, she nodded her head, as if what he had said was more sensible. Life breathed wisdom into her soul upon these words, "Trust in the Lord with all of your heart and lean not upon your own understanding. In all of your ways acknowledge Him and He will direct your paths." Eve blinked her eyes and rubbed yellow pus from them, as her mind began to sober. Terror ran through Serpent's tiny body. Within a flash, he stretched himself completely around her and gazed deeply into her eyes. Tenderly, he convinced her of the real life she had been cheated out of. "Love Him? Trust Him?" Tilting his head away from the sunlight, he gently squeezed her body.

Then he beckoned it to focus upon his eyes, which had become mirrors. She saw her reflection transform from "ordinary" to glamorous. Secretly, he placed two green berries in her palm and continued, "Love you. Trust You. Be your own god."

Adam dropped two perfect red apples and ran to his wife's side. Surpassing the speed of light, the serpent unwrapped his body and perched himself on a branch to observe. He spoke one last time to Eve, "Be your own god." These words resounded in her soul as whispers, seducing her repetitively. Well aware of his effect, he muffled his chuckles in order to hear the confusion about to be unloaded.

"What's this all about Eve? Why are you here at this tree talking to a strange serpent? I don't understand." Eve laughed and explained it simply, "Serpent found the perfect fruit for our salad." Revealing the berries she placed one into his hand and paused one last time to the sound of the Tree of Life. Adam fooled by her silence thought she was listening to the words, which tried to save her, "Children, God is Love. Love is patient. Love is kind. Love does not envy. Love does not vaunt of itself. Love is not proud. Love does not seek her own." As though it was a soothing balm, she glided the fruit back and forth over her lips. Then suddenly popped it into her mouth. "Eve!" he shouted "What are you doing?! You can't eat that! You'll die!" She swallowed it. "I'm not dead. You won't die either. It's just another fruit. Look at your berry Adam. Doesn't it look good?"

For the last time, he looked at the berry as it sparkled in the glory of the bright new sun. For the last time, he saw the merry serpent stand upon legs. For the last time, he gazed into the eyes of his naïve wife. For the last time, he saw the garden as home. All of these things happened for the last time because for the first time he would disobey God. Without a formal declaration, Adam and his wife would redefine Life and Love. Life would be fast, competitive and pompous. It would require hard labor, exchanges, disputes and wars to possess the necessities. Instead of having one God and one command, life would become complicated by having many rulers and laws. Life would involve pain, diseases and famine. Love would be self-fulfilling. You could find its corrupted version in any common or forbidden place. Love would be the term used to justify lust or futile ambition. All that is good would be inevitably mingled with evil.

Sunbeams danced upon Adam's tongue as he opened his mouth to receive the fruit. As his mouth began to close, the light ran from him as dusk of the day. Closed and dark the chewing began. The poison spilled over his tongue empowering it to lie, destroy, kill and steal. Then trickling down his esophagus, it scraped the tender lining, which would become ulcers to his offspring. When it landed in his belly, it immediately absorbed into the wall. In a flash, it dispersed powerful toxins throughout the body, which altered the human DNA. He lost control of himself in a violent seizure as his mind and body transformed. Terror, confusion and a swarm of new thoughts and emotions flooded his soul. Perfection had been mutated and its strange characteristics: diseases, sin and poverty would plague future generations. The obedient trait in his character became deformed, twisted with pride and double mindedness. Every man and woman after Adam would desire to be their own God. Their first inclination upon every life issue to follow would be to mock God. They'd have to learn to trust Him by faith or consequence. Sewing and reaping would go beyond the planting of plant seeds, but every kind of seed. Filled with darkness, Adam experienced fear for the first time and so did Eve. At that moment, their eyes opened and they understood what death really was because it had become a part of them. They were wrong and they knew it. The Tree of Life spoke for the last time to them as they hid among the fig trees, "My children, perfect love casts out all fear"

Farlinda, I hope you understand what I am implying with this story. Re-examine how you run the people in your life and the operative word is "run." Please know that love is assertive, not domineering. It guides and doesn't dictate. Love allows for choices (even if they are wrong) and it's always there to rebuild what poor choices have destroyed. Your fear of rejection has caused you to reject true love .Your frustration with rejection causes you to fight back with manipulation and control. I implore you to give God your heart. Let Him fill it with His love and quench your thirst for true life. Farlinda, always remember, love does not seek her own.

Gretchen, by the stripes of Jesus you are healed! Be whole mind, body and spirit. God had increased your heart to adopt a child. You want a child to give someone hope, but this *child will be the sign of hope for your second chance. Your past is behind you. You will no longer have to buy back your life, because He is giving you a new one.*

Shantise I don't question your faith, but Jesus said, "My sheep hear my voice, and I know them and they follow me." Take the time to hear what the Lord is saying to you. If you miss the Lord, it will be like having Ishmael, a true blessing (His acceptable will), but not God's perfect will.

My daughters, abide in faith, hope, and love, these three; but the greatest of these is love.

Tearfully, Farlinda closed the book. "That's it. That's all she wrote." Her sisters were quiet and pensive. "I don't want to dictate. So what shall we do now?" Relieved, Gretchen sighed, "We had originally planned to meet here tomorrow to read the both wills. We have done half of that. How about we all just go home, get some rest and come back tomorrow evening. I don't know about you, but Mama's diary gave me a lot to think about." "Yeah, me too" Shantise said glancing at her watch. It was 6:20. She had about two and half hours to solve the mystery of Chain and Mann. Farlinda wanted to explore the closets in Mama's office, but her tired back screamed, "No!" "All right then, shall we come back at five o' clock tomorrow?" Farlinda asked diplomatically. "Five O Clock" Gretchen and Shantise responded in unison. Within five minutes they had cleaned the kitchen, secured the house and drove off in three different directions.

Chapter VIII

Facing Reality

7:01 PM

"Jamel, it's Grete. We need to talk tonight, call me back"

"Uncle Gene, this is Shantise. Do you know anything about someone named Taurus Mann?"

"Farlinda, I thought you'd never get home! The kids are watching TV and I have a surprise for you"

"What's up baby? How did things go at your mother's house?"

"Taurus Mann, the singer and producer, died last month"

"You didn't cook again did you?"

"It was good. I learned a lot. Can I come over? I have some things to tell you."

"He Died! I thought I met him today. Are you talking about the guy from Orbit Records?"

"I didn't cook, but you're gonna love this! Close your eyes and hold my arm."

"I see you in the driveway. Just come in. The door is open."

"Shantise, Taurus is dead for certain. Tell me about this person you met today"

"We're in the dining room! Marshall, you said you did not cook! I have eaten already! I'm warning you"

"Jamel, do you love me?"

"TJ introduced Velvet and me to these two guys from Orbit, Chain and Mann. They want to record us."

"Open your eyes!"

"Of course I love you, with all of my heart"
"Chain! The other guy was Chain! What did he look like? Did he have a car?"
"Oh thank you Lord! A catered dinner! Marshall, thank you! Thank you!"

"Unconditionally?"
"Tall dark skinned man who looked like he's mixed with an Asian. Bald headed with scars on his neck."
"The kids have eaten and Jenny's keeping them in the den for us. We need this time alone."

"Unconditionally."
"He rode off in a white Monte Carlo"
"This is the best Mother's Day present!"

"First thing in the morning, I'm making an appointment with Amelia Covington. I need the help."
"How soon are you kids planning to meet with them again?"
"Ah! Look at his table! Steak, lobster, baked potato, asparagus, heaven!"

"I'm proud of you."
"Tonight. They're taking us to Hollywood."
"This is only the beginning."

"There's more. Are you sure you love me unconditionally?"
"The Taurus Mann you met is an imposter and Chain is a

dangerous criminal we've been tracking."

"Oh my god, Marshall, you bought me a dozen red roses! "

"Just say it Grete."

"I'd better warn TJ and Velvet!"

"Yes, twelve roses, but I'm sorry to give you just one ring."

"There was someone else. Actually, there were others... three"

"Don't, but since you're in the middle, what do you say to helping us shut down a prostitution ring?"

"Mr. Taylor, are you asking me to marry you?"

"Really Gretchen, three?"

"A prostitution ring! Really?"

"Really, will you marry me?"

"Really."

"Really."

"Really."

Chapter IX

Night

Shantise met Detective Eugene "Gene" Harris at the Krispy Kreme on West Broad Street. As he came in, she noticed him rub his belly when he glanced at the "hot doughnuts" light glowing in the window. He sat facing her with a serious expression, but she tried hard not to laugh at him. "Ok, Tise, tell me everything you know about Chain and Mann." She reported her exchanges with the gentlemen and went on to share about the brief encounter with officer Rojas. "He gave you a break? Rojas? That's not like him at all." Harris said rubbing his head thoughtfully. "You said they looked and smelled like the same person?" "Yeah and that scared the hell out of me! I've never experienced anything like it! What's going on here? Taurus Mann is dead and I met two people today who look like him. That's some crazy shhhh!" Shantise stopped herself half way between her would have been a cuss word. She remembered that not only was Harris an officer and her elder, but he used to be her father's best friend too. Endearingly, she and her sisters called him Uncle Gene. Cupping her mouth as if she had swallowed an egg, she exhaled an embarrassed but sincere, "I'm sorry." Harris chuckled at her resistance to let it go. He remembered how Henry used to talk in the bowling alley and Justine used to tell him to keep the bowling words out of her house. A leaf does not fall too far from the tree.

A shapely young woman dressed in Levi's blue jeans, a tight yellow tank top and black high top Chuck

Taylor's left the counter. She had big brown eyes, pouty red lips, and light brown skin. Short black curls dressed her rounded head, giving her the appearance of a living doll. Carrying a tray of doughnuts and coffee, she came to their table and sat. She pulled a dirty khaki backpack off and placed it on the empty seat beside Shantise. Her glamour length sculptured nails with yellow and black designs looked like bumble bees on steroids. Two long trains of fake gold bracelets ran from her wrists to the middle of her forearm. Gaudy rings wrapped seven of her fingers. Two of them were brass knuckles. Her ears were adorned with large gold tone bamboo hoops.

Shantise could imagine hearing Vita and Jewel saying, "Praise the Lord!" when she spotted the tiny golden cross dangling around her neck. Five "bees" wrapped around a cup and placed it in front of Shantise. The bees went back to the tray to get Harris's cup. "Thanks Summer!" Harris beamed as he reached for a hot glazed doughnut. No longer able to contain herself, Shantise laughed out loud. "Uncle Gene you are such a stereotypical cop!" Summer laughed too as he devoured the doughnut in two bites.

Harris shamelessly stuffed another doughnut before drinking some coffee. White crème pasted his lips like crust. Tiny pieces fell on his shirt and a few landed in the coffee. "You ladies know that I always have crème in my coffee." They both shrieked at the sight of him. Summer handed him a napkin, "Harris, you're a mess!" Then she turned to Shantise to introduce herself, "Hi, I'm Detective Trina

Summer, Harris's partner." "Partner?" Shantise asked doubtfully. "You mean, you're a cop too?" "Ah, yes and were police officers not cops." Summer corrected. She pulled a small laptop from her backpack. "Harris, here is what I found on Taurus Mann. He was born in Baltimore, Maryland on April 30, 1975 to Lucio and Felicia Villas. Nathan and Elizabeth Mann adopted him immediately after his birth. They named him "Thomas." His performer name is Taurus. Now what I found to be really interesting is that his birth certificate indicates that he was one of a multiple birth."

"That doesn't surprise me. I had suspected he was one of two or more. How many were born?" Summer shook her head, "It doesn't say." "Alright then, look up the birth record of our very own Officer Simon Rojas." "What does Rojas have to do with Mann?" Summer puzzled as she typed "Simon Rojas" in the search box. Harris did not answer, but waited expectantly on the revelation of his theory. Shantise and Harris remained silent as Summer typed and clicked through what must have been several pages of information. She frowned and grunted as she quickly scanned Rojas's birth certificate and a few other records. After about five minutes of silent research, she leaned back on her chair and exhaled, "Unbelievable! They are brothers! Harris is this what you wanted to confirm?" He nodded and said, "Now tell me what you found." Summer massaged her neck and began, "Rojas was also born in Baltimore on April 30, 1975. His parents, Lucio and Felicia Villas, named him Roberto. His first triplet, had no name at birth, but was given an identification number. The statement under the number said the name would be determined by adopting parents. I guess the unnamed one was Thomas. The other triplet, Ricardo Villas, was adopted a week later by David and Anne Hamilton. They renamed him "Richard." Roberto was adopted later that same day by Angelina Rojas and was given the name Simon!"

Harris clapped his hands, and then shook a doubled fist, "Yes! Now that is good work Summer! Get access on the DMV records on all three!" He picked another doughnut off the tray and took a regular sized bite. Slowly he chewed to relish its taste. Pride faded from his countenance and his expression became stoic. Shantise watched the two of them transform in her mind from Uncle Gene and the street kid to Detectives Eugene Harris and Trina Summer. A higher level of respect had risen for them. These two were experts in their field. Judging by Summer's brass knuckles and Harris's nearly invisible gun he had strapped on his side, they were not to be played with. "I'm almost there. Hang on a few seconds for the masterpiece." Summer told them. She slid and tapped the mouse a few more times, then turned the screen around to show her findings to Harris and Shantise. "Oh... My... God!" Shantise gasped as she looked at the findings. On three driver's licenses, side by side, were the faces of Thomas Mann, Simon Rojas and Richard Hamilton, identical triplets! "Shantise did you see any of these men today?" Harris asked. "Yeah, at least two of them!" she answered patting her chest. Summer grinned and whispered to herself, "It's yellow dress time!"

133

"Okay, young lady here is where you help us." Harris said. "Where did you say these guys plan to meet you and your friends?" Shantise's throat became dry as the danger she sensed earlier manifested itself more and more by the minute. Her body trembled as she answered the question, "We're supposed to meet at Velvet and TJ's townhouse at eight o clock." "What's the address?" Summer asked. "5499 Fire Wood Lane" Shantise's head dropped and tears formed in her eyes. Her friends were in trouble and there was not anything that she could do about it accept wait until Chain and the Mann impersonator were caught. Harris had explained how dangerous the situation would become as they approach the suspects and make the bust. He told Shantise to go home and not make any kind of contact with her friends until he called her. Reluctantly, she obeyed.

Five police cars parked in various places within one block of Fire Wood Lane. Harris and four other officers sat in a work van just across the street. The faded green van appeared old and insignificant: no hubcaps on the tires, rusty fenders and a thin coat of dirt covering its exterior. Though common on the outside, inside was a state of the art bugging system. The undercover agent connected to it parked in front of TJ and Velvet's door and knocked.

"Hi, I'm Roxy!" the undercover agent announced to a puzzled Velvet. "I'm supposed to meet a guy named Chain here!" she said with a smile as big as Texas. She took off her backpack and tried to walk in the town house. "Are you with

Orbit?" Velvet asked, blocking her. "Oh no girl, I used to be a receptionist at the Veteran's hospital and now he's taking me to Hollywood for an office job in Orbit Tower!" Velvet was immediately jealous of her. Roxy had the face, hair, and the body of feminine perfection, all wrapped up in a yellow Spandex mini-dress. "Congratulations" Velvet responded dryly. She turned slightly to call TJ. "Can I come in?" Roxy asked. "Yeah, I guess so" Velvet opened the door wider for her entrance.

TJ came zooming by with two suitcases and dropped them on the curb in front of Velvet's Escort. He returned with Mann, hugging on his shoulders. "Look who's here Velvet! It's my man, Mann!" He was flushed, sweaty and extremely jittery. Abruptly, Mann pulled away from him and said, "Kid, I'm not who you think I am. You guys are in a lot of danger dealing with Chain! He's not from Orbit! In a few minutes he's going to knock on the back door, have you whisked out by his partners and thrown into a van." Roxy interrupted "You talking about that fine Chinese looking brother Chain?" Mann shook his head, "Yeah and we gotta hurry. Come with me now!" Velvet grabbed TJ's side, trembling. Shocked and frightened, neither of them could move for a minute. "I said let's go now! These men are going to pump you with Mystic and put you on the street somewhere! You will not know where you are. The only thing you will know is your pimp's name. You will not care about how many men screw you, where your next meal is coming from or whether or not your dreams of becoming a star will come true. The only thing you will give a damn about is how soon you'll get your next fix! Now do you want to stand here, get drugged and raped for life or get the hell out of here with me!"

Roxy tapped her chest with bumblebee nails and asked, "You got that Harris?" "Yeah, we got it, now get them out! Backups are on the way!" TJ and Velvet clung tighter. "You're a cop?" Mann asked. In utter disgust, Roxy glared at him and answered, "I'm Detective Summer and you have a lot of answering to do Rojas! Now get out!" she ordered. Before he could utter in his defense, six officers rushed through the front door. Two of them pushed TJ, Velvet and the Mann impersonator out of the townhouse. Roughly, they ordered them to get into another unmarked police van. The four remaining officers hid themselves behind furniture. Summer slammed the front door, pulled a bulletproof vest from her backpack and strapped it on. The officer behind the hutch tossed her a camouflage print helmet, which she quickly fastened to her head. Stretched out on the sofa, she looked like a fantasy dancer dressed to play "army."

In the van, Harris grabbed the impersonator by the shoulders and demanded his questions be answered. "Rojas! Why are you involved in this case and going undercover without authorization?" Before answering, the impersonator looked at TJ and Velvet sorrowfully "I'm not Rojas! My name is Richard Hamilton. I got involved when I first saw them run the game. Two weeks ago, they took a waitress named Cheri out of the Medallion Society to sign a contract. No one had seen nor asked about her since. We members are used to having our girls quit and never come back. I noticed that one of the guys looked just like me. Another waitress told me the guy who looked like me was someone named Taurus Mann. I did not say anything because I knew that Mann had died a few weeks ago. This Thursday, Chain had mistaken me for Rojas and told me he had a new target, a boy and some waitress friend of his. He described a girl from the Medallion. I had never seen her before because she works weekends and my hang out hours are during the week. That is when I learned that they were white slave traders. I played along, but only to stop Chain from victimizing another kid." Harris gave Richard a "You Idiot!" look and said, "Why didn't you just call us, instead of trying to be a hero? You could have been killed!" He sighed in frustration and called his partner. "Summer, the guy I have is Richard Hamilton. Looks like you will be dealing with a good cop gone bad! We are gonna lock up one of our finest tonight, Officer Rojas. "

A few minutes later, Chain and Rojas, came through the back entrance. Then their partners had backed the van to it and opened the doors to easily shove their victims in without being seen. Five teen-aged girls were laid on the van floor. They had been knocked out by Mystic. Chain licked his slip-on golden grill. He wore it whenever he felt confident that he would soon be getting paid. "Hey ya'll! TJ, Velvet, Shantise, we are here! Let's Go!" Summer called back, "They ain't here yet, but I am!" Upon entering the living room, Chain and Rojas drank their eyes full of the sexy girl spread out on the sofa. "Umph, umph, umph! Simon, this is what you call a money machine!" Chain moaned while punching his partner. "Hey, I'm Roxy, Velvet's friend!" She said playfully. Judging the lusty eyes and watering lips, Summer knew her game was working, so she poured it on more. "Shantise got engaged today, so she isn't going with ya'll. Now, I can sing and rap better than her. So that means ya stuck with me, Diamond Roxy!" she purred and wiggled her hips seductively. Chain drew closer, "Miss Lady, you want to be a star?" "Hell yeah!" she sang, flashing a huge smile. Summer had played several roles to catch criminals in the act and enjoyed doing it as much as arresting them afterwards. Passing for a naïve, nineteen or twenty year old was by far a favored role played by this thirty year old, seasoned police officer. As "Roxy," she could momentarily escape the adult life and revert to a time when she could chew bubble gum, wear outrageous clothing and sport daring hairdos. After spending a little time "on Barbie vacation," the woman returns, startling the guilty party and having her second rush. Summer had never met Rojas. The thought of revealing her true identity to a "dirty cop" would be the source of her joy for weeks to come.

"You gonna take me with you guys too?" Summer squealed. "Yeah, Come on!" Chain smiled as he grabbed her arm to get up. "Wait a minute, I need to go back home to get my things." Summer said sweetly, while pulling toward the front door. "You won't need a thing. We got that all covered" Chain sharply answered. "No but I need to bring my wallet!" she pulled towards the door again. "We don't have enough time for that. I told you we got you covered. Come on!" Chain pulled her again. "Chill out Chain! Be nice. The lady just needs to relax before she's ready to go." Rojas said reasonably. Attached on the side of his belt was a mini holster of needles filled with toxic cocktails. He pulled out a needle filled with Sleep Mystic and headed towards her. Roxy's charming girlish voice was suddenly replaced with a full-grown woman's bark, "Officer Simon Rojas and Luther Chain, you are under arrest for attempted kidnapping, unlawful use and distribution of narcotics, identity theft and prostitution!" Chain and Rojas froze as officers appeared around the room with guns pointed at them. Chain's partners were pulled from the van and arrested.

Shantise answered her phone on the first eight notes of Mariah Carey's *Hero*. "Tise, this is Uncle Gene. They're all right."

Chapter X

Dawn

A soggy cooked noodle was awkwardly laid upon a hot rock. This mismatched pair of food and stone had been forced to exist together. Easily devoured, dried or spoiled, the fragile noodle covered the rock as if it were its equal. A stone picked from the campfire that burned all night was put aside to cool. Thoughtfully, the camper's experiment would begin. He dropped the cooked noodle on the stone and waited for the impossible to occur. Hypothesis: As the rock cools, the noodle thickens and doubles in size over and over until matches the size of the rock. Contents of the noodle undergo a strange metamorphosis and transform into stone.

A passionate fire of anger, shame and regret had burned that night. Truth had unsealed the can of venomous worms and poured them out on the table for the lovers to examine. One by one, they identified each worm and tossed them into their fiery argument, until they were all gone. For the second time in twenty-four hours Gretchen, lay her head upon the chest of Jamel. This time, he too was exhausted. Their bodies ached with the pain brought on by the unveiling of Gretchen's lifestyle and all of its sickening details. Learning that her running days were over and she was ready to settle, brought no comfort to Jamel. The decent woman he loved avoided commitment for a good reason. She had been a player and he had to deal with that.

Jamel remembered the words of his grandfather, "God doesn't give you any more than you can bear" as

Gretchen dished out the details of her soon to be over relationships. He repeatedly said this to himself as she told him about her appointment with Doctor Phillips and the tests she ordered to check her findings from Gretchen's last gynecological exam. Now both of them feared the results would be a malignant tumor in her uterus. To make things worse, Garrett called Gretchen on her cell during the argument several times but she did not answer. After six calls, he left a text, which read, "Call me NOW this is extremely urgent!" She asked Jamel to let her go into his bathroom to return a call because of its nature. He snatched the phone and saw Garrett's name. His answer was "Hell no! You call this weak punk ass player right here! You said you wanna keep it real with me Grete! Call him now!" Pressing the phone back into her hand, Jamel began to pace the living room floor.

She collapsed on his sofa, crying and shaking when she called back. Gretchen knew she was in love now. There was no wave of her hand, no telling him where to go or what to do with himself. She could not fight him because this was not a game and she would do anything to keep her man. Jamel had exploded with cursing and crying all over his feelings for her. No man had ever allowed his feelings for her to be fully exposed as he had that moment. He was the man who would love her, protect her, and die for her. Those were the words he used when venting his every thought. Though burning in anger, he did not reject her. He momentarily stopped pacing and waited to hear what Garrett called "urgent." Jamel eased her palm upward and pushed the speaker button on her phone. The drama began again.

"Hi Muffin" Garrett said in a weak voice. "I have some news for you and it's not so good." Irritated she snapped, "What now? I am at Jamel's house and I told him about you and the others. He is very upset! So what's your news?" Garrett took a deep breath before dropping the bomb. Bitter weeping proceeded out his mouth instead of the speech he had prepared. He sounded very feminine. Jamel's wide eyes shot at Gretchen, "What's up with the girly crying? Is this guy gay or bisexual?" Garrett cleared his throat and answered, "Down low bisexual and I'm sorry to tell you this way Muffin. You know we have a special friendship and we swore to be truthful to each other, so here goes..." As he took in his second deep breath, Gretchen buried her face in a sofa pillow awaiting her next surprise. Jamel resumed his pacing. Garret sadly reported, "Grete, Muffin, I'm HIV positive." The pacing stopped, the phone fell to the floor, but Garrett continued talking; "Now you probably don't have anything to worry about because we were always very careful in our times together. It's just that I think you should get tested to be sure that you're still negative."

Determined not break down again, Jamel walked silently into the kitchen and poured himself a glass of Chardonnay. "God didn't give me more than I can bear," he said out loud to himself. "I can handle this mess. If God brought me to it, He will bring me through it." He had brought Jamel into Gretchen's life for a reason. Jamel is the strong man who could bear her trials and tribulations as if they were his own. He is the one who would love her unconditionally for the rest of her life. Gretchen could be heard sobbing in the living room and faintly Garrett's voice called her name several times before he hung up. Without taking a sip, the Chardonnay was poured down the sink. "Oh God! What do I do now?" Jamel cried to Heaven. The words "HIV positive" stung his soul and all emotions were put in the shut down mode. Completely numb, he was unaware of his feet treading the floor as he made his way back to Gretchen. He could not even feel his arms as he slid her body on top of his. Dazed, he wrapped his arms around her. They stayed on the sofa all night in each other's embrace. Jamel, the stone was removed from the fire and a soggy cooked noodle was placed upon him. The camper awaited the transformation.

Chapter XI

Day

Farlinda's Day at the store had been long and stressful. She worked two more hours than planned and was now rushing to pick up Florin from an afterschool program. The ten minute drive to Amanda's Day Care had been the quietest moment of her day. Her feet were swollen and she hurt all over. The hot patch had just begun to penetrate the achy muscles of her lower back. She parked in the handicapped spot in front of the door and crept inside. Horace and Dina, the director and his assistant, greeted Farlinda with a fake smile, as she signed the pick-up form at the entrance. After she had walked out of an earshot, Horace corrected Dina, "She's not Mrs. Taylor. That's Florin's last name. Her name is Miss Silva and she's about to have the third baby by this man she lives with." Dina whispered back, "Isn't her oldest about fifteen or sixteen years old?" Simultaneously, Horace rolled his eyes, swiveled his neck and clicked his tongue as he prepared to leak out more juicy gossip. "He is and that's not all. You know that perfume store where I buy my lotion?" he asked. "Yeah, what about it?" Dina said. "She owns it and she uses her money to pay for her boyfriend's education. You know he will not marry her. He is just using her until he gets what he wants. Now you know that's a sin and a shame!" Surprised by his remark, Dina replied, "A sin and a shame? Wait a minute sister-girl; don't you live with an unemployed man that you are not married to? What do you call that?" Horace was about to give her a piece of his mind when Farlinda returned from a classroom with Florin. "Bye Florin. Bye Miss Silva" they sang in unison, sporting the same façade they wore upon her entry. She was not fooled by their phoniness, but politely ignored it and said, "Good day."

"Ah!" Farlinda groaned as she lay back on the car seat. "What's wrong Mommy?" Florin said rubbing her mother's hand. "I'm supposed to meet Auntie Grete and Auntie Tise at Grandma's in a little while. You wanna come with me?" Florin cheered "Yes! Yes!" Farlinda gave a weak smile and said, "I was hoping you wouldn't have said that. I wanted to take you home, become too tired to leave and stay there." Florin squeezed her hand and encouraged her, "Come on Mommy, you can make it. Just take a little nap at Grandma's before we leave. If you're still tired, Auntie Tise can take us home." She gave her a proud look and nodded in agreement. Little Florin's ability to push and persuade would be relentless until she achieved her desired end. Some day in her near future, the princess would become a queen just like Farlinda.

At 5:00, she parked behind Gretchen's BMW in front of Mama's house. Florin dashed out to meet her aunt Gretchen on the porch. "Auntie, I miss you!" said squeezing her waist. "Silly, you just saw me last week at Grandma's funeral." *"But* I didn't *hug you then bec*ause I was so sad about Grandma. I never ever see you anytime and I miss you!" She hugged her tighter and Gretchen broke. "Florin you are so right about that. I haven't been a good Auntie, but I'm changing that," Having disappointment written all over her face Shantise wanted to question her about her lovers. Gretchen read her mind and said firmly, "Yes Auntie Grete has already begun to change some other things too. Do not judge me Tise. I've had a rough night." Feeling a bit hypercritical, Shantise apologized, "Last night was a rough one for me too. I nearly lost my two best friends." "What happened?" Farlinda noticed the look of confusion in Florin's face and sent her to Mama's office to play with the rag dolls. Shantise told them the crazy story about two siblings who didn't know each other, who impersonated a dead man who just happened to be their long lost triplet. She told the how she and her friends had been tricked and set up to be victims of white slavery. Then she told them about Uncle Gene's beautiful partner, the undercover officer who arrested one of the brothers. During the story Farlinda, had made peace and love to the sofa pillows. Gretchen stood before her in awe, "Tise, I'm so sorry, but thank God you guys are ok!" She hugged her tightly and said "Well, don't give up on recording. Remember what Mama wrote to you." Shantise nodded yes and both of them laughed at Farlinda's inappropriate responses to everything they said. They knew she was half-asleep during the whole conversation. The only sensible thing she did say was "Thank you Jesus" which shocked them.

He stood four foot nine, in a thin, wrinkled body. His bald brown head looked like a shiny little Milk Dud. Thick rounded eyeglasses were worn on his clean-shaven face and a heavy scent of Old Spice poured out from under his collar. A long sleeved white shirt, black loafers and slacks with suspenders were his regular business attire. Shantise snatched the front door open after it had been banged on four times. Irritated by the lack of respect, she wondered who could be knocking so forcefully without saying, "Open up this is the police!" Expecting to see an oversized brute, she covered her smile at the sight of the tiny big man. Mr. Lawrence Turner, attorney, had arrived.

Slightly offended by her stifled laugh in his face, Mr. Turner greeted her first in a dry tone, "Good evening young lady. Is there a Farlinda Silva here?" Shantise pushed a giggle to the back of her throat and choked out a bubbly response, "Good evening" Mr. Turner grunted and walked pass her. Gretchen frowned at her silly baby sister and showed him to a comfortable living room chair. Farlinda sat up right, and then introduced herself and sisters. He wasted no time after the introductions to reading the will he had filed in his brief bag.

Mr. Turner began, *"To my dear daughters, Farlinda Silva, Gretchen Silva and Shantise Silva, I give you all of my earthly possessions. More important, I leave you my love and wisdom. Hopefully you have read the diary, my informal will, and know what's going on through my mind at this time. If you haven't, take the time to read it. You can find it in the chest under my bedroom window. The key is in the back of the diary itself.*

To Shantise I give you the opportunity to respond as mature adult. You have fussed at me more than either of your two sisters about your "lack" of freedom and me treating you as a child. So here is your chance to prove your ability, not to me but to yourself. My gift to you is a test and you will know if you pass or fail by evaluating the outcome. If you squander this gift, there is nothing I can do about it. You cannot be rescued, but you can plan wisely. Shantise, you have this lovely house and property with all items inside except the things specifically given to your sisters. You are the beneficiary of my two supplemental insurance policies, which should be worth $175,000. You have the burden of paying my final expenses, which is my electric bill, cable, water and phone. I have paid off all of the credit cards, the house and the car. That should leave you with a good sum to do as you wish. Just remember, if Hollywood does not work out, you still have a place to call home.

`Gretchen, you seem to think that I loved you less than your sisters. I admit, you were taken for granted and often overlooked, but it wasn't intentional. For most of your child and teen years, you tried to show me how special you are: making good grades behaving well and doing everything you were told to do without complaining. Gretchen, you were a perfect child, almost maintenance free. You thought that your works were unseen, but they weren't. I loved and needed that sweet gentle child. Then you grew up and away from your family. Every time you used to speed away from here to go home or wherever, I regretted not spending more quality time with you. In your adult life, we both tried to make up for time loss. I tried to bond with you more and you tried to pay yourself back for *what you didn't get as a child. Please forgive me and let the past go. My Dearest Gretchen, I give you all of my jewelry, keepsakes, crystal, silver, and china. These are my most precious possessions. Please remember how precious you are to me when you use them. I'm also giving you my wedding album and first picks for any other family book. These are to remind you that you belong to a loving family who will always be there for you.*

To Farlinda and her children I give all of my other financial accounts: investments, savings & checking, cash, and car. Just in case Marshall stays at Big Fat Burger for life, I'm blessing you and my grandbabies. There should be enough money to live on for a couple of years if anything unexpected should happen to you or the grown child. Sweet heart you have worked so hard for what you have, but you never established a plan B in case something life altering happened. So this gift is your second chance to have a nest egg for you and some money for my grandbabies to go to college. Mr. Turner or his associate will be giving you the key to a locked box in my room which has all of my accounts (yours and Shantise's) and a personal letter for you."

Mr. Turner gave Farlinda a copy of the will and a key he had pulled from his pocket. "Ladies, you had an extraordinary mother. I am grateful to have known her. Use these gifts wisely." They thanked him and with that, he left as fast as he came.

The room remained silent moments after he left. They had been given a blessing and a challenge, all at the expense of their dear mother's life. Gretchen passed tissues to her sisters after she had helped herself to a handful. Florin returned bewildered, "Why is everybody crying?" Farlinda waved for her to sit by her side and said, "We all just miss Grandma. Sit here a minute. I need a hug." Florin moved quickly but carefully to her mother. She gently placed her arms around Farlinda's shoulders and rested her head upon her neck. Tiny Streams flowed from hazel eyes as Florin tried to squeeze the hurt out and love into her. Watching this touched something in Gretchen and she was not ready to feel it. Instead, she shook it off and said, "I didn't see a locked box. Did either of you see anything?" Shantise said nothing, but went upstairs to Mama's room. There on top of the chest of drawers was a large metal locked box. She had seen it the day before and would have tried to open, but the scent of Rapture had taken her attention away from it.

Shantise returned to the living room and placed the box on Farlinda's lap. She unlocked it and sorted out the documents. After giving Shantise her papers, she began reading the letter to herself. Allowing a "respectful" fifteen seconds, Shantise broke the silence, "Can we hear it too?" Gretchen gasped, "Tise, no!" Farlinda, waved them both off and rose, easing Florin from her side. Without another word, she floated into the office still reading the letter. Her daughter and sisters followed curiously. Farlinda stopped in front of a pair of closet doors. The letter fell to the floor. She bit her bottom lip before wringing out the tears, which had clouded her vision. Then she slowly untied the gold ribbon, which held them together. She froze staring at the door. "Open it" Shantise implored. "Ah, you two go first" she whispered back, pointing to the other doors tied with ribbons. Shantise and Gretchen tore off the ribbons and pulled open the doors. "Oh! Oh my god, this is gorgeous!" Shantise cried beholding the most beautiful formal gown she had ever seen. "This is incredible!" Gretchen said breathlessly. She had the identical gown in her closet. Both gowns were on mannequins. They had cards with their names on them pinned to the chests. "Come on Farlinda. You can do this" Gretchen encouraged her. She hugged Farlinda and held her tightly as she said to Shantise and Florin, "Open the doors please." They all beheld perfection, Mama's masterpiece, the wedding gown of Farlinda's dreams. Her eyes filled with tears once more and she spoke to heaven, "Yes, Mama, we're ready now."

Epilogue

"A New Day"

It had been a month since Gretchen and Jamel had the fallout over her past relationships. They had decided to separate for a while to think and sort things out. In the meantime, Jamel operated like a workaholic! He denied himself the pleasure of attending any social event, even lunch with his employees. Work would distract him from doing his part of the "thinking and sorting things out" with a woman he wasn't sure that he could trust." Gretchen began seeing her counselor and did spend a lot more time with her family. Shantise made some decisions which made her feel like a real adult. She split from TJ and Velvet so that they could move on with their passion to become a duet singing mostly love songs. Then she signed a contract with Christian Records, cleaned out my house and put a *For Lease* sign in the yard. Farlinda and Marshall had been preparing for their wedding on the weekend. Yes, yes, my buds did blossom, but that is not all that happened.

A few weeks ago on Thursday, Shantise went with Gretchen to have some testing done. They had spent most of the morning testing, crying, and praying. Dr. Phillips would have all of her results just before noon. Gretchen was so scared she did not want the doctor to use words when she gave her the news. "Just put one finger up for cancer and two for HIV. With your other hand, give me a thumbs up or down beside them. Please do them slowly one at a time, so I won't freak out."

As they waited for the results, Gretchen told Shantise all about Jamel and how she was hoping he would give her a second chance after therapy. It seemed unreal for her to learn about Gretchen's past and now see her as a new woman in love. Some day my baby girl would be rapping about what she had been witnessing: God's power to change people's lives. But nothing could have prepared her for what was about to happen next. Gretchen's purse made a jingling sound. It was Jamel calling. "Hi Grete" he paused and continued, "Look, I've been doing a lot of praying...Nobody's perfect and it wouldn't be fair to expect that from you... A really nice guy told me that." Gretchen smiled and said, "You mean God?" "No, but I can say that God sent him. He delivered a UPS package to me this morning. It was Garrett. He told me everything and now I understand... I am sorry... No matter what the tests results are, just know that I love you and I am here for you always." She wiped her tear-drenched eyes just before saying "I love you Jamel" and hung up.

Just after that, Dr. Phillips returned. She put up one finger with a thumb up. My babies exhaled and prepared for the second finger. She raised two fingers and ... Praise the Lord, she put a thumb up again and my babies began to shout! Then Dr. Phillips cleared her throat and wiggled a third finger. She gave Gretchen a mischievous grin and put her thumb up. I will tell you what that meant later when I update you on Farlinda.

Shantise's little friends, TJ and Velvet, did not turn out to be so bad after all. TJ had given up selling CDs and Velvet quit working for the Medallion Society. They sang,

"The Prayer" at Farlinda's wedding and announced their new entertainment business, Love Songs Inc. on the wedding program. Master Raine Taylor, Marshall's best man, stood proudly by his father. The debonair Richard Hamilton strolled down the aisle with the lovely Shantise on his arm. Next in line was the most handsome couple I had seen since Henry and I were a pair, Jamel and Gretchen. She glowed like a Christmas tree and it was not just because she had her man back. Both of them were excited about Dr. Phillip's number three she carried in her womb. They all stood nicely before the altar when the song "Seasons" began. Florin marched in pouting and throwing handfuls of flower petals on the floor. She loved the dress I made her, but hated hoop slip Farlinda made her wear under it. That poor baby looked like Little Bo Peep! Most of the guests got a kick out the angry flower girl. Cameras and phones all over the sanctuary were snapping shots of my grandbaby's tantrum. Then Farlinda came in. My sweet Farlinda was biggest, prettiest bride that ever walked down the aisle of Grace Christian Church. Gene, Henry's best friend, proudly escorted his "niece" to the groom. Just before they made their first step into the sanctuary, I heard him whisper to her, "It's about time!" She just laughed, knowing this was the last time he would encourage her to get married.

My soul is at peace with Marshall Taylor. I had misjudged him too. It turns out that he graduated and earned his Juris Doctor at the end of May. He will be taking the Bar next Saturday and he has some interviews lined up with law firms. The service was beautiful and Pastor Edwards ended it as usual, giving the husband a family bible. He pronounced them husband and wife, they turned to leave and Farlinda was struck by the greatest labor contraction ever!

Henry and I have trained them. Our work is done and now Lord they are in your hands.

"Train up a child in the way he should go: and when he is old he will not depart from it."
-Proverbs 22:6

Questions for Study Group or Devotion

- What reasons, other than the ones stated, do you think Justine chose to share her convictions about her daughter's lives in the format of stories written in a diary?

- Justine had her own opinions about the people in her daughter's lives. Discuss the accurate and inaccurate judgments she had made concerning their character.

- Do you believe that Justine was legalistic? Why or why not?

- Who were the heroes and heroines of Mama' Diary? Who are yours? How did they influence your life path?

- How well did the Silva family know each other? Were their relationships with one another ideal, weak, or typical?

- What do you believe God wants for families? Did the Silvas live according to God's good, acceptable, or perfect will?

- Birth order is a factor in the development of personality and self-image. How did birth order affect the personalities and self-images of Farlinda, Gretchen and Shantise?

- Mama's diary is about choices. What influences and tests challenged the sisters to choose the path to a more abundant life?

About the Author

    Bridgette D. Williams, a native of Glen Allen, Virginia was raised in a busy home of writers, poets, and musically talented siblings. At a young age, she discovered within herself that same love of creative writing and music. After High School, she joined the Hard Rocks Ministry, whose sole purpose was to spread the gospel of Christ though rap, singing, hip hop style dancing and teaching. During her years as "Baby Fresh" (artist name), she pursued her B.A. in Social Work at Virginia Union University and the University of Notre Dame. Also during that time she joined Lighthouse Christian Center where she has worshipped and served in various ministries the last twenty-two years. In 1996, she earned her M.A. in Teaching at Regent University. Today she is a public school teacher and also serves as Director of the Lighthouse Christian Center's performing arts ministry, "Signs and Wonders."

Bridgette expresses her love and adoration for God though the ministries of drama, mime, poetry and storytelling. Her desire is to give Him back everything that He has invested in her for His Glory. She says, "We are all so full gifts, talents, and abilities, that we would cheat ourselves out of the best chapters of our lives, if we choose not to use them.

Mama's Diary is a novel about these kinds of choices. Added to that, we must be guided by faith, hope, and love in order to make those choices without hurting ourselves and others. My prayer is that everyone who reads this novel will be encouraged to choose the abundant life that only our God can give."

TO ORDER ADDITIONAL COPIES OF "MAMA'S DIARY"

please forward your check or money order (plus shipping and handling) to:

Bridgette D. Williams
P. O. Box 1007
Sandston, VA 23150
(E-mail): bridgettew66@yahoo.com
(Website): www.serenityconnection.com/

Qty.	Item	Unit Cost	Total
	Mama's Diary	14.95	
	In Virginia add 5% sales tax	Subtotal	
		Shipping	
		Grand Total	

<u>SHIPPING & HANDLING:</u> *Please add $3.00 shipping for each item ordered. For orders placed outside of the U.S., add $6.00 shipping per item.*

<u>Ship to:</u> Organization:

_____

_____ _____ (Mr./Mrs./Ms.)_____

Last Name   **First Name**

_____

Street Address

_____, _____ _____

City   **State**   **Zip**

Phone: ( ) _____ E-mail:_____

THANK YOU FOR PLACING YOUR ORDER!!!

CPSIA information can be obtained at www.ICGtesting.com
Printed in the USA
BVOW020642101011

273230BV00003B/4/P

9 780983 909071